Zulus, Girls & Videos

or . . .

trying to be COOL in a nearly black suit

Zulus, Girls & Videos

or . . .

trying to be COOL in a nearly black suit

John Farman

Piccadilly Press • London

To the memory of Rover

First published in Great Britain in 2001
by Piccadilly Press Ltd.,
5 Castle Road, London NW1 8PR

A catalogue record for this book is available from the British Library

ISBNs: 1 85340 653 8 (trade paperback)
1 85340 658 9 (hardback)

1 3 5 7 9 10 8 6 4 2

Printed and bound by Creative Print and Design (Wales),
Ebbw Vale

Cover design by Louise Millar
Design by Mark Mills
Set in Caecilia Roman 10pt

Hi, my name's Joe Derby. Most of the time I see my real life as a bit of a disaster movie, with me as the hero and the villain all in one. Let me tell you all about it!

ZULUS, GIRLS & VIDEOS
Starring – Joe Derby
Directed by – Joe Derby

THE CAST

ZOE DERBY – *my sister*

My big sister Zoe is twenty-two going on forty. Ever since she was about sixteen she's acted as if being young was some sort of a crime. To be honest, I suppose if you saw her for the first time in the street, you might think she was not too shabby – tallish, blondish, good legs, larger than standard-issue boobs and a not bad face – six out of ten, some might say. Funny how wrong you can be.

Mind you, it's quite difficult to look at your own sister as if you've never seen her before, so I had to be told this by my mate Merlin (see MERLIN). I suppose it's possible she might turn some guys on – she obviously does her fiancé Graham (see GRAHAM) – but I find her about as sexy as my dog Rover (see ROVER) – which is just as well. What is it called when blokes fancy animals (or their sisters)? Anyway, let's list her good points first.

Umm . . .

OK, let's list her bad points.

I think it's fair to say that if I were the Invisible Man (or Boy) she couldn't pay me less attention. She doesn't even see me most of the time. The Invisible Man was such a cool film. This old scientist guy plays around with drugs until he finds one that makes him disappear.Just think of the fun you could have. Just think of the girls you could watch undressing. I reckon I'd be permanently stuck in a corner of Merlin's sisters' (see MERLIN'S SISTERS) bedrooms.

Sorry!

Zoe talks to men as if it's a known fact that they all fancy her. It's not just guys of her own age, it's all men – young, old, rich, poor – even my mates. You should hear her. She puts on this yucky butter-wouldn't-melt-in-her-mouth, cutesy voice that makes my skin crawl. Blimey, she even attempts a faint lisp sometimes.

Yuk, yuk and double yuk!

Mind you, the poor little girl act obviously works with some of them. Poor Merlin reckons he's always dreaming about her and I have to tell him off for his gross lack of judgement. I wonder if it's the same sort of thing as guys having rude dreams about parking wardens or Cherie Blair.

Zoe's bedroom is like something out of Whatever Happened to Baby Jane, the dead scary film where a wrinkly old ex-movie star played by Bette Davis, refuses to grow up and ends up doing her sister in. To see my sister's room with her menagerie of fluffy animals, shagged-out Barbie dolls and ghastly out-of-date pop posters, you'd think her development had been mysteriously arrested at thirteen – and as for those soppy teddy bear slippers – the only one who gets turned on by them is Rover (but we won't go into that now).

Since Zoe got engaged to Graham (see Ludicrously Out-of-Date Customs in Modern Times *by Joe Derby*) she's been impossible.

GRAHAM BUNT – *Zoe's fiancé*

To spend any time actively hating Graham Bunt would be a waste of my already overloaded brain space. He's everything I can't bear and apparently everything my parents (and presumably my sister) can. For a start, he drives one of those spazzy little Japanese sports cars, the sort that hairdressers love. It's bright red, of course, which I suppose makes him rather dashing – if you're into the Mr Bean school of dashing, that is (God, don't you hate Mr Bean?).

You should see Zo when he pulls up outside of the house. She skips down the front path like some dimbo bimbo from some ghastly Sixties pop movie like Summer Holiday, waving her stupid arms about and making sure all the neighbours see her. Blimey, I'd wear a bag over my head if I was going in that thing, especially if it involved sitting next to Mr Podgeworthy. Oh yes, I forgot to mention, Graham's well on his way to serial fatdom, even though he's probably got a willie the size of a prawn (sorry – a shrimp). Me and my friends call him 'Barry at Mr Buy-Rite' because he always looks as if he's raided a department store when the sales are on. That really naff term 'smart casual' could have been invented for him.

Graham has perfected crawling to an art form. When he's with my parents, you could be forgiven for thinking it was them he was marrying as well as Zo. I suppose he is when you come to think of it. He's certainly round our bloody house enough. He obviously thought the whole thing out like a military operation.

Here's how **Operation Zoe** goes:

Stage 1: Smarm your way round the parents – flattering the mother's appearance and the father's garden.

Stage 2: Offer them a discount at the store you work in with a dumb plastic card that says they're special. (Graham, by the way, is Assistant Manager in the Homes Department of Somers, our local department store.)

Stage 3: Tell them that they are the parents you wish you'd always had.

It'll be game, set and match before you know it. My gran used to call it 'getting your feet under the table'. Creepy Graham's managed to get his whole fat body under ours.

The best thing is that the sleazebag knows that I've rumbled him. He knows that I see through the flowers he always brings for my mum and the cuttings and seeds for Dad (I'm sure he nicks them from his own parents' back garden). He knows that I know that when he offers to dry up after Sunday lunch, my mum would never let him.

Barbara Derby – *my mother*

I reckon when my mum gets herself tarted up, like she does when her and Dad go out, she actually looks better than my sister (although that's a bit like saying the Queen's better-looking than Princess Anne). Poor Mum, she must sometimes feel like she's being seen out with her uncle – Dad always looks such a catalogue man. There's him in his blazer and beige slacks, cream shirt, knitted tie (he sometimes wears bright socks, if he's feeling daring) and, of course, suede shoes (always suede shoes) – standing next to her in her shorter-than-strictly-necessary black dress, showing more-than-strictly-necessary cleavage and quite sexy high-heeled shoes. They look like Beauty and the Double-Glazing Salesman. Now there's a movie waiting to be made . . .

At forty-three, Mum doesn't exactly look like mutton dressed as lamb, more like rather attractive old lamb dressed as slightly younger lamb – a bit like Mrs Robinson in The Graduate *– sexy but, dare I say, maybe looming ever so slightly towards her sell-by date. The reason she does it, I reckon, is because she was never allowed to when she was young.*

I reckon my mum is far cleverer than my dad, but like Zoe, married practically the first man that asked her (what other excuse could there possibly be?). My gran once told me that in those days girls were told they were 'on the shelf' by twenty-five and would live the life of a sad spinster. So what's Zo's excuse, I ask myself? Just think, if

Mum had hung on, my dad could have been someone groovy – not that groovy people ever spent a lot of time hanging around Northbridge.

My mum has never really worked and spends her time doing all those things that women do when they've got nothing to do – Meals on Wheels, Women's Institute, the church flowers once a month, collecting for baby Africans outside Sainsbury's – you know the sort of thing.

I sometimes think she could be the woman in Shirley Valentine. That's the film where this ordinary housewife, from somewhere ghastly like Bolton, meets a Greek waiter on holiday and leaves her old man to shack up with him. The main trouble with that movie (apart from it being a load of sentimental old poo), was that the Greek waiter was played by a bloke called Tom Conti, who was not only about as Greek as I am, but a damn sight worse-looking (I think) than the husband she left behind.

DEREK DERBY – *my father*

The Adventures of Derek Derby – The Novel, were it ever to be written, could be the shortest book in the world – even shorter than Zoe and Graham's Guide to Stylish Living or Rover's Book of Personal Hygiene. From what I can make out, he was exactly the same as he is now, right from a kid: never answering his parents back, never bunking off school, never wanting clothes or anything else his parents didn't approve of, and never ever thinking of being anything but a Quantity Surveyor like his own dad. Quantity Surveyors, by the way, are people who count and measure things . . . I think.

Like Mum, Dad never went to college, never had a flat with his mates, never took drugs or got pissed, and probably never ever slept with anything apart from his Rupert the Bear hot water bottle before he married my mum. When he's not playing golf, or doing stuff to the house, or mucking around in the garden, Dad spends a lot of his time in the shed.

I suppose his shed's like my room – a refuge from the world. I saw something on TV once that said that men need their own space much more than women and that women often take it personally when their old men hang out for hours on end in sheds. Anyway, Dad must be doing other things apart from fiddling around with the model steam engine that he's been building for years (if progress had been down to him, we'd still be on flipping horses). For a start, whenever I go in there (I nicked the spare key, by the way) it stinks of fags (Dad packed up 'officially' five years ago) and, apart from that, where do you think I 'borrow' my magazines from? Pinching a man's girlie mags, by the way, is one of the safest crimes in the world, I reckon, as no one would ever admit to owning them let alone report them missing. My mum would have Dad's guts for garters if she ever found them.

MERLIN LABARDIA – *my best mate*

Merlin Labardia comes from completely different stock to my lot. Jane and Tony, his mum and dad, were hippies and still are in a way. To be fair, they had no real chance of being anything else. They met, so Merlin told me, at a commune in Somerset where their parents lived next to each other in matching psychedelic Post Office vans. It's only because Merlin's father really made it big-time and became a really successful artist that they (that's Merlin's mum and dad, his two sisters and him) aren't there now. These days they all reside in fabulous shabby splendour in one of the biggest and bestest houses in Northbridge. It always reminds me of the Bates Motel in Psycho. For me, going round to Merlin's place is like a penguin visiting a wombat's house – it's so different. Theirs is a completely sorted world where none of the rules that we all know and hate exist.

Merlin's one of the coolest guys I know. He calls his mum and dad Jane and Tony, stays up till he's tired, eats when he feels like it and has a room that looks like a set from The Addams Family (except the cobwebs are real) and is allowed to do more or less anything he likes with his hair. At the moment, as we're still on summer holidays, he's got those sticky-up dreadlocks, but he's pretty sure they'll have to come out when we go back to school. Actually, I think they look daft. They're OK on black people (I suppose) but look a bit silly on us whities.

Merlin has an obsession with girls' chests. The girls he fancies could be ugly enough to frighten pets for all he cares, but as long as they've got large, well-formed boobs he forgives them everything.

So why is Merlin my best friend?

Well, I could never tell him, but I think he's the funniest, honestest, coolest person I know. Most of my other friends pretend to be different, but when it comes down to it they're all into the same sort of things – fast cars, blonde bimbos, football and 'EastEnders'. Merlin's different, he lives in a world of his own and anyone that doesn't like it can sod off. Best of all, out of everybody he knows, he likes me best. That's fine by me.

SKY AND JADE LABARDIA – my best mate's sisters

Look, I know you can't really fancy your own sister, but it beats me how Merlin can begin to lust after mine when he's got two of the wickedest-looking babes living under the same roof. Sky and Jade (OK, I admit they're dodgy names) are sixteen and seventeen and are almost too gorge for me to even be in the same room with – I nearly always have to put a cushion or something on my lap (if you know what I mean).

I think Merlin's dad must have a touch of foreign in him somewhere (especially with a name like Labardia) as both girls look a bit gypsyish, with big black hair, big dark eyes and the sort of lips that seem to have been made for snogging (or anything else you can think of). Sky, the eldest, is slightly taller, with long slim legs and a body that you can picture with your eyes closed. Jade is ever so slightly shorter, maybe even prettier, and has slightly larger boobs which she is extremely careless about covering up

13

(I'm extremely pleased to report). Not only do the sisters look good, but they talk good too. It's so cool. They've a way of making you feel that everything you say is witty and dead intelligent. That's the good news. The bad news is that girls of only a year or so older than you usually trawl around with eighteen- and nineteen-year-olds, even if they do appear to like you.

Who am I kidding, anyway? Even if I did get my hands on one of them I'm not sure I'd know what to do. I know the theory backwards, but I'm a bit behind, to say the least, on the practical. Anyway, which one would I choose? I suppose realistically I'd stand more chance with Jade as she's younger. Talking of which, I got the video Ten Things I Hate About You last week. In that the guy has to get the elder sister, who's a bit of a beast, fixed up before he can move in on the younger one. I'd be happy with either (or both).

One of my best fantasies is that one day, when I'm a famous movie director, I'll be able to offer them both parts (well, one at a time – nudge, nudge). Unfortunately (for them) they'll both fall hopelessly in love with me and have to fight it out between themselves. Sorry, girls – that's life.

ROVER – our dog

If they had a category at Crufts dog show for the coolest pet, our dog Rover would walk it. I reckon he's the canine equivalent of Merlin in every way except he doesn't seem that bothered about the size of girls' chests. Actually, he doesn't even care if his current fancy is even a dog (as Zoe's teddy bear slippers will testify). Rover lives in his own crazy world of eating, sleeping, farting, having it off with anyone or anything that will let him ... and dreaming. I'm not sure what he dreams about but I've got a terrible feeling that I wouldn't want to know if I did. Best of all, in a house full of aliens, Rover is most definitely an officer and a gentleman, far preferring *The Kingdom of Joe* (my bedroom) to being with the rest of my tragic family.

And finally . . . me!

JOE DERBY – Yours Truly

You already know my name's Joe Derby. I'm just fifteen and I share a house with my mum and dad and sister Zoe – oh yes, and Rover, our long-haired, short-witted dachshund.

So, what do I look like? Well, if you can you imagine a young, slightly better-looking version of a cross between Brad Pitt and Leonardo DiCaprio? – forget it. I don't look anything like that!

I'm fairly tall, 5ft 7ins (or 1.7018 if you want me in metres) with ordinary brownish hair. I suppose I'm not that bad-looking on a no-spot day, though I really wish I had to shave a little more often than once every fourteen years. Merlin's one of those blokes that was shaving at about three and now has to get up and do it in the middle of the night in case his beard suffocates him. I reckon it's because he's got a touch of the old foreign blood in him (but hates it if I say so).

Although I haven't got that bad a body, I'm not remotely athletic. Me and Merlin are known as Les Deux Slobbonis at school because we waste more time thinking of ways to get out of sport, than we would if we actually did it.

As for girls, me and Merlin are as interested as any other red-blooded perverts, but neither of us has gone the whole way yet. I've kissed a few, but nothing of any great quality, and not really using tongues (or anything else come to that). Merlin says he once got this rather large girl, Jane Barraclough, down to her bra and knickers, but just as she was about to lose them, she suddenly came to her senses and kicked him out. Still, it's further than I've ever got. Mind you, that's if he's telling the truth. Merlin's not a stranger to the odd porkie, especially where the ladies are concerned.

My ideal girl would be a cross between Jade and Sky with a bit of that singer from the Corrs thrown in (by the way, I can't stand all that diddly diddly music, but the girls are real babes).

The way I dress is casual to the point of ragged. I'm so understated clothes-wise that people selling The Big Issue offer me money and the council once launched a fund during Beautiful Northbridge week to keep people like me and Merlin off the streets. I'm joking, but seriously we both think new clothes suck (unless someone did a new, old-looking T-shirt saying NEW CLOTHES SUCK).

Oh yeah, and my favourite food's bacon sandwiches.

I live (if you call this living) at thirty-nine Onslow Drive, in the

16

dreamy and exotic suburb of Northbridge, just on the edge of London. I say on the edge, but it might just as well be on another planet as far as I'm concerned – it's so boring.

I have the second smallest room in the house next to the lav and it's dead groovy – it's my refuge from the Dreaded Derbys and a nasty virus called suburbitis which threatens all humanoids that are trapped in Northbridge too long. I spend hours upon hours in here, trying to keep the rest of them at bay. I always think my life's a bit like living in that old film Zulu – you know, the one where Michael Caine and a bunch of rather hot British soldiers are holding this garrison in Africa somewhere, against thousands of ever-so-cross natives.

Mum and Dad, are the cross natives, by the way – always trying to get past my door. OK, maybe not to kill me, I'll admit. Worse! Their mission in life is to tidy me up! Well, they say they want to tidy, but we all know what they're really after. They're after my vast library of Dutch pornography and the two tons of drugs (ha!) I keep under the bed.

If I'm Michael Caine in this version of the movie then Rover is my second-in-command. He's fast asleep at the moment, but always ready, at the bottom of my bed.

Scene 1

The Kingdom of Joe Derby.
Sunday 1.30 p.m.

ACTION:

Hang on a minute, I think I hear a Zulu hovering around.

'Joseph, are you in there? It's me, your mother.'

Damn, I thought it might be that Jennifer Lopez again, she usually calls round about this time for a quick snog. I decide not to say a word, but shove my headset on so that I'll be able to say I couldn't hear. Rover, ever poised for action, opens one eye, yawns, and begins to lick himself in a place where only dogs can. I look at the door and notice that the door handle's beginning to turn slowly.

Blimey, *Zulu*'s turning into *Psycho*.

Have I locked it? Yes, thank the Lord. I've got three copies of *Razzle* open on the bed, one of them with Donna from Doncaster, my current fantasy girlfriend, sprawled across the centre spread.

'Joe, dear, I know you're in there. I saw you going up. What are you doing?'

On the scale of things your mother needs to know, this rates about minus seven, so I keep my mouth shut. But it's no use. Dammit, Rover old boy – we're trapped. Shucks! We can't even shoot our way out this time.

'Sorry, Mum, I'm just putting the finishing touches to the time machine I've been making out of Sugar Puffs packets. You'd better be quick, I'll be in the far distant future in ten seconds flat.'

The Time Machine, by the way, was one of my favourite movies. It was all about this bloke who spent years working on this brill contraption which could make him go back or forward in time at the pull of a lever.

'Don't be silly, I want to talk about the wedding,' says Mum somewhat impatiently. 'Zoe's getting worried that you'll do something silly and let us all down.'

'She should know all about being silly and letting people down,' I reply, 'marrying Graham, King of the Geeks.'

'Now don't start all that again. She could do far worse. We all think Graham's a very nice young man. (All think? ALL THINK?) He's got a good job, a nice car . . .'

'. . . and the worst haircut this side of the Russian army. C'mon, Ma, he's a grossoid, we all know it really. You're just glad to be getting Zo off your hands. She's been awful since she's been engaged.'

If getting married is naff, I reckon getting *engaged* takes the mega-naff prize of the millennium. What does 'engaged' actually mean, anyway? Does it mean that you promise you won't do *it* with anyone else before the big day? Seeing as I'd bet next month's pocket money that neither Graham or Zoe have done it with anyone else anyway, I fail to see what they're so scared of. I reckon both of them should count themselves lucky.

All Zoe does when she's at home these days is moon around the house with fabulously intellectual magazines like *Hello* and *OK*, ringing boring photos of boring rich people's boring houses with her boring index finger, saying that they're just like the way her and boring Graham are going to have theirs. Who's she kidding? If Graham does up houses anything like he dresses, they'll be living in a third-rate version of an MFI showroom before you can even say DIY.

I turn to Rover.

'You're lucky, mate, they don't allow your kind at weddings, otherwise she'd be having a go at you.'

Rover stops licking and looks at me balefully.

God knows why I've got to go to their wedding on Saturday week. Family solidarity, I think Mum called it. If that's not bad enough, she now says she wants me to go out with her to buy some *proper* clothes so's I won't show the family up.

SHOW THEM UP? What about *ME*? I ask myself. What about *them* showing *me* up?

Rover is just about to speak when the Zulu representative outside beats him to it.

'I don't want you showing us up.'

There! You see? She said it.

'What about you showing *ME* up?' I almost shout.

'Don't be so dramatic. It's only one day and it'll be nice to have some proper clothes.'

What, in the name of Fred Flintstone, ARE proper clothes? If she and my father had their way, they'd have me looking like an escapee from the church youth club, or that bloke in *The Talented Mr Ripley* – sensible trousers, sensible shirt and sensible shoes made of proper shiny leather with laces and everything. Now she's telling me that Dad's prepared to fork out for a suit.

A suit! Me in a *suit*? Oh, pleeease!

I can just see it – bank-clerk grey, with a shiny lining and some poncy label saying *Charles of Slough* on the inside pocket with DRY CLEAN ONLY in little letters underneath. Oh yes, and that's just the beginning. What do suits go with? You're right. All together now – TIES! What is the point of ties?

Anyway, I think I know what this suit business is all about. It isn't just the wedding, is it? Oh no. I reckon it's part of a much bigger conspiracy to smarten me up and quieten me down. Jeez, I'd be richer than Bill Gates if I had a quid for every time my old man's told me that he used to be just as rebellious as me when he was my age.

'*Ah yes, once I'd realised that it was better to accept the way things are, rather than trying to change everything, I never looked back. The world opened up for me. You'll never get anywhere with your attitude, young man, believe me.*'

'Sorry, Papa,' I wished I'd said, 'but if you'll pardon

my interruption, that's a load of pure, undiluted *shiten-hausen* (as they say in Germany).' Tell you the truth, I don't think my dad Derek ever really was a real teenager. I think he just slithered into grown-updom overnight, like a butterfly from a chrysalis, except he did it back to front . . . he's now a full-time chrysalis.

Anyway, who gets married any more? It's so uncool – it's so what people did ages ago – it's so . . . so Zoe!

'Look, are you going to open the door or aren't you? I'm not going to stand here arguing.'

The Zulus are still out there!

I almost invite my mother to *sit down* and argue, but think the humour might be wasted. I shove my girls under the mattress, push Rover off the bed (she always says my second-in-command's a health risk), open the door and notice immediately that her steely gaze leaps over my shoulder and penetrates the gloomy interior of my sacred domain – the fabulous and mysterious Kingdom of Joe.

'How many cups have you got in there? We'll need to open a factory soon to keep up with you.'

'Mother dear, did you really come up to talk pottery or shall we stick with the wedding of the century?' I say, blocking her view from the pile of old socks and pants festering in the middle of the floor.

'Are you going to come with me on Saturday to buy this suit or not? We've only got thirteen more days, and I've got enough to organise without having to worry about you.'

'Oh no, not thirteen days! You didn't say thirteen days, did you?' I try to go pale. 'I've got some bad news, Mother. I've got this strange woozy feeling. I think it's the very first stage of that mystery bug that's going about. You know, the one that comes to a head in about – um – thirteen days.'

'Joseph (she always calls me Joseph when she's cross or wants me to do something) – what's the matter with you? Don't you want to be with your sister on her special day? You must know how much it means to her.'

'Oh come on, Mother – get real, she'd rather have another poncy tier on her poncy wedding cake than waste money on me.'

'OK, if it's strong-arm tactics you need, then you shall have them, my lad. Let me think.'

She pauses and thinks.

'Right, young man. If you don't play ball with us . . .'

'. . . then you won't let me have any more cups. Gosh, *Herr Commandant*, you strike a hard bargain, but alas, what need of cups have I when dying from this fearful plague?'

'Will you be serious for one moment? If you don't make an effort, we'll cancel your subscription to the video club.'

Ouch! That really *was* a score for the Zulus. Right below the equator. Even talking about it is deeply serious.

Let me explain. If you haven't guessed already, ever since I've been a tiny kid I've been a complete cinema junkie – a filmoholic – a movie maniac – a video voyeur, you name it. I don't know why, but all I ever think about is films – adventure films, cop films, sci-fi films, westerns, you name it. I don't like sport, clothes, collecting things or very much else – just films (oh yes – and girls).

Mum and Dad put in for a special deal that was on offer at the local video shop last year that allows me five (videos, not girls) a week – it was my last birthday and Christmas present combined. I've actually been working there for most of the summer holidays which has meant I also get the first chance to buy them cheap when they're about to be taken off the shelves. The bloke who runs it quite likes me because I can tell the customers what most of the movies are about. He's even offered me a Saturday job when I go back to school.

Films are all I live for and why (for want of any better reason) I don't want to work in Dad's poxy office or any other poxy office come to that. If I'm not working in movies by the time I'm, say, twenty-five, I shall – no, I *must* end it all. I'll even make a disaster movie of myself doing it. My current favourite is:

THE WHEEL OF DEATH
starring Joe Derby

Story so far:

The London Eye is on fire. A beautiful babe, played by Cameron Diaz, has left her baby spaniel in one of the pods which has now ground to a stop at the top of the wheel. I'm an escaped convict on the run from the law and they're right behind me.

I burst through the police cordons and, in full view of the police and the TV cameras, scramble up through the smoke and flames until I arrive triumphant at the top. Waving to the crowd, I grab the dog and plunge – a hissing fireball – a hundred metres into the River Thames. The puppy survives but I am just an unrecognisable but heroic frazzle. The rest of the film consists of flashbacks about how misunderstood I was, narrated by my poor dad from a monastery, where he's gone as penance for treating me so badly during my short, tragic life. Cameron Diaz, by the way, never gets over it and builds a shrine to me in her bedroom.

What do you think?

'For the last time, are you going to come to buy this suit?'

It's Mum and I'm miles away at the scene of my death.

'I guess you got the draw on me, Ma'm,' I drawl – a personal tribute to John Wayne, my very best cowboy. 'I guess I'd better come kinda quietly.'

Scene 2

The lift at the Northbridge Arndale shopping centre.
Saturday 10.30 a.m.

ACTION:

'What level did we leave the car on?' my mum asks as soon as we get out of the lift.

'Search me, they all look the same.'

'How are we going to find the car when we want to go?'

'Search me, they all look the same too.'

'Seriously, Joseph, how are we going to find it?'

'I don't know. Can't we just choose one roughly the same size and colour? No one'll notice.'

'If you can't say anything sensible, I'd rather you kept quiet.'

'J for joke,' I mutter under my breath.

I think going shopping with your mother must be like being taken to McDonald's by a vegetarian. This morning started badly. Every time I go in Mum's car, I swear it will be the last. Have you ever seen those daft *Herbie* films, the ones about the VW Beetle that tears around with a mind of its own? Well, being in a car with my mum is similar. Only she can leave a series of multiple pile-ups in her wake, while never even scratching her own car. I used to wonder why there were always ambulances whizzing past. Now I know they were ferrying the dead and injured to the local hospital.

OK, I exaggerate, but seriously my mum IS the world's very worst driver. In that film *Dr Jekyll and Mr Hyde* there's this doctor who invents a potion which can turn him into a psychotic monster at will. My dear mother's the female version. If anyone dares toot their horn at her she goes off on one.

'MUM! Mind that cyclist, you're heading straight at him.'

'Well, he should be in the cycle lane, shouldn't he?'

'There isn't one.'

'Well that's hardly my fault, is it? I blame the council.'

We've reached the multi-storey car park, which smells reassuringly of pee.

What is it about the people in shopping centres that makes you want to phone God and force him to admit he's made a right cock-up of the human race? Do you remember the bar in the first *Star Wars* – the one where all the aliens and mutants meet? Northbridge's Arndale centre must be where they do their weekend shopping. Talking of aliens, I wonder what people from another planet would make of these places?

'Aha, comrades, here we are at last. This must be one of the nerve centres of these strange people. Wow! Aren't they hideous!'

Where else on this planet do you get so many people like this all in one place? Sad wrinklies, sitting round the garish fountain while poisoned water tinkles down on the bloated chips and burger boxes; small children being slapped senseless for being small children, and fat people – everywhere there are fat people, tons and tons of fat people – all mooching around to an odd medley of pan-piped music and a dweeby girl singing 'Somewhere over the Rainbow', while collecting for homeless hedgehogs.

'We'll start here, this place is really "with it",' says my mum, who could shop for England.

'I thought so,' I say. 'I could swear I just saw Naomi Campbell and Kate Moss over in the half-price knickers department.'

World of Fashion, where we're going for my suit, is one of those retail chains that sell everything from socks to suits throughout the length and breadth of Merrie England. Should you be careless enough to lose the trousers you bought in Edinburgh, you can buy an identical pair in Plymouth, which is one of the reasons why everyone over thirty in this country looks the same. But *I'm* not over thirty – so what in the name of Mr Buy-Rite am I doing here? I ask myself. If I'm not careful I'm going to look just like Austin Powers in *The Spy Who Shagged Me*.

'Do you have any suits to fit a tallish boy of fifteen?' my mother asks the scrawny assistant who's long given up trying to look busy.

'Over there – Young Adults,' the gum-chewing beauty drawls, pointing a hideously overgrown fingernail with a fake diamond set in the middle.

'Since when have I been a *young adult*?' I groan.

'Perhaps you'd rather be an *old child*,' says Mum, which takes me a bit by surprise.

'Ah, these look rather smart,' she says, as we get to where the girl was pointing.

SMART! What is it about that word SMART that makes me want to chuck up? I reckon if ever you were doing a crossword and you needed a five-letter word meaning the opposite to COOL, you wouldn't have to look much further than SMART.

I trudge gloomily to the changing booth with a dark grey suit that Mum's picked out. Apart from having legs that I can practically fold up and pin to the back of my knees, it seems to fit pretty well. Blimey, I think they were thinking of an American basketball team when they designed it, or the lady in the trouser-making department had her mind on her tea break.

'All right,' I say, stumbling back, the legs dragging behind me, 'can we go now?'

'Hang on a minute, don't you want to try the others?'

'Why?' I answer. 'I didn't want the flippin' suit in the first place, why should I like any of them better than this one? Please, Mum, do we have to do this? I look such a cretin.'

Mum yanks me about like a rag doll, almost trying to make it *not* fit, but has to admit that, apart from the length of the legs, it's remarkable – the damn thing fits like a glove. A sad, boring glove admittedly, but a glove all the same.

I can see the way all this is going. This is just part one of Mum and Dad's plan to make me a regular Zulu like the rest of them. Dad was droning on about it just last night.

'Look at that Lionel from number seventy-two. Five years ago he was kicking around with no ambition, mooching about like a reject from the Oxfam shop. Now he's Assistant Junior Office Manager on fifteen grand a year.'

Yeah, and he'll probably be a serial killer by the time he's twenty, I thought to myself.

'If you were to apply yourself,' he went on, 'and look a bit more respectable, I might even be able to get you some work experience.'

EVEN ME! Yippee! Oh thanks, Daddy, I thought. A once in a lifetime chance of a glimpse into the wonderful and awesome world of Quantity Surveying! It's like Christmas come early – I so can't wait.

'Is this the one you want, then?' Mum asks, dragging me back towards the rails of clothes.

She's obviously feeling cheated at the prospect of buying something without trying on half the shop first – and then the next shop, and then the next, and then . . .

Aha! I smell a trap. This could be a trick question. If I say yes, it will imply happiness maybe even tinged with gratitude, and if I say no, we'll be here till bloody Christmas.

'I think it will be the perfect complement to such an auspicious and memorable occasion,' I say in my poshest voice, suddenly wondering if my true future might be in diplomacy rather than the movies.

The price makes me wince. Just think of all the stuff I could buy with that money – all the movies I could see, all the posters I could pin up throughout my kingdom.

Scene 3

The Kingdom of Joe Derby.
Tuesday 10.00 a.m.

ACTION:

Me and Rover have just had breakfast and I've called Merlin to see if he wants to do some more work on our movie.

'Hi, Joe, how're you doin'?'

'Dead busy, can't stop – watching movies mostly.'

'Like what?'

'I got round to *Chicken Run*. I missed it first time round.'

'What do you think?'

'All right if you're into Plasticene poultry in a big way, but I reckon it got a bit boring. I know it's supposed to be a redo of *The Great Escape* with hens – but after an hour or so of hundreds of those silly cluckers all yapping at once, I began to lose the plot.'

'I know what you mean. It all ends up looking and sounding the same if you're not careful – and they weren't. I reckon *Toy Story 2*'s better. Bring back Wallace and Gromit, I say. Want to come round?'

'Yeah, OK.'

I put the phone down and look at Rover guiltily. 'Sorry, mate, I guess I'll have to leave you to face the Zulus alone.'

I would take him with me, but he always starts whining when he gets within a hundred metres of the Labardias' house. You'll soon see why . . .

Scene 4

The Labardia house.
Tuesday 11.00 a.m.

ACTION:

'Hi, Joe, come in. Have you had any brekkie?'

It's Merlin's mum, Jane, looking just as mad as ever in a long purple caftan with tiny mirrors sewn on, and what look like butterflies attached to ribbons hanging from her mauve dreadlocks. Normally I'd think it was a bit tragic, but she's so brill I'd forgive her anything.

'I had something at home, thanks – is Merlin about?'

'He's upstairs in his room, do you want to go up?'

The Labardias' house is wicked – for a start you could put most of our downstairs in their hallway. But, if you begin to think of the sort of place that well-off people normally live in – don't! Everywhere you look there's something weird and wacky. Right in the middle of the hall, with the family's jackets and coats draped over its arms, is a huge stuffed bear wearing a shiny pink plastic cowboy hat and sunglasses (*naturellement!*). Real seagulls (dead, too) swing on invisible wires from the ceiling, which is dark blue and covered in stars. Every few minutes cuckoos spring out from one or other of the twenty or so cuckoo clocks all set at different times. There's one of those big wooden screens like you get on seaside piers with paintings of fat ladies – the ones where you put your head through the holes where their heads should be, to have your picture taken. All round the walls, in huge gilt frames, Merlin's dad's done fab paintings of everyone in the family, including their cat Gandalf, to look like old masters – dead cool, I think.

Best of all, at the end of the hallway is one of those joke mirrors you sometimes get in fairgrounds that make your head look five times bigger and your legs six times shorter. I wonder if they do one for willies? (Perhaps not.)

Merlin's door has been made to look like the entrance to a dungeon, with metal studs and a small hatch with bars across it, which can only be opened from inside. I pull the rope and the bell clangs ominously. The little door in the big door opens and Merlin's face appears. As I said before, he's now got dreads, but with his long face and pointy nose, he looks more like Rover than my mate.

'Hi, Joe, what's going on, man? Hang on, I'll let you in.'

I wait a while and listen to the scrabbling of bolts being pulled back and chains unfastened. Merlin's got this big thing about horror films and has tried to make his room as much like a cross between a castle in Transylvania and an undertaker's parlour as possible. All round the place are the family's ex-pets going back years – all stuffed to look like they're asleep, which is what scared the wits out of Rover – and there's a real skeleton just inside the door holding a sign, presumably for female visitors, saying *All clothing must be left here.*

'How did the suit buying go? Was it gross? Want a cuppa?' he asks as soon as I'm in his huge room. Can you believe, Merlin's got his very own little kitchen where he can make cups of tea and toast and everything! Talk about COOL! Life's not fair – when I think about my parents I reckon I must have been what's called 'an accident of birth'.

'Cheers, mate – two sugars,' I say. 'Buying that stupid suit was worse than gross, I looked like Prince William by the time she'd finished. Then, just when I'd got the full kit on, my silly moo of a mother suddenly came over all misty-eyed and kissed me because she reckoned I looked so grown-up and wasn't her little boy any more. Jeez, I think she'd really prefer I'd stayed at five.'

'Did you have to get a shirt and tie and all that? Did you?' he asks, wide-eyed.

'The whole bit. It really sucked. We even bought proper shoes and socks.'

'Sounds more like you're going to a fancy-dress party,' he says, laughing. 'How much did that lot set her back? Was it a lot?' Merlin always asks questions twice.

'Too bloody much, if you ask me. I keep thinking of all the stuff I could have bought with the dosh.'

Merlin's tall and skinny and only ever wears black, which makes him quite difficult to see at the far end of his dim dungeonette. He's also into movies big-time like me, by the way, but says that he'd prefer to be a film star than a director – each to his own, I suppose. The sort of films we like, other people find a bit weird. Stuff like *The Blair Witch Project, X-Men, Clerks* and *Being John Malkovich*. Merlin's current favourite is a fairly old film called *Flatliners* in which a group of American medical students, led by Kevin Bacon, experiment with death by nearly killing one another just so they can bring each other back at the last minute to tell the others what it was like. Cool or what!

For ages now (well! a couple of weeks) we've been working on our first feature, which we're going to shoot on Merlin's dad's dead flash video camera. He's even got a thingy that does editing.

He hands me a mug and says, 'Only five days to go to the big day – tee hee. How's Zoe feeling? Do you reckon her and Graham are going to actually *do* it on Saturday night? Do you reckon they will?'

What a revolting thought. Imagine that tubby toad all over anyone, let alone my sister.

'I wish it was me,' says Merlin, almost wistfully.

'I always thought you were a pervert. Mind you, I'd even prefer you as a brother-in-law to Graham. At least you . . .'

'Ooh! By the way,' Merlin butts in, 'I forgot to tell you, you know that outfit that Jade sometimes works for on Saturdays, that does weddings?'

'Yeah,' I reply slowly. I have a horrible sinking feeling that I know where this is going.

'Well, they're the ones doing Zoe's on Saturday at the hotel, and she's going to be a waitress. What a gas – eh?'

'Oh sure,' I say. 'I so want her to see me dressed like a fully paid-up prat. Hell, as if it isn't going to be bad enough.'

That would be most definitely it, I thought. Any credibility I ever had, straight down the pan with a lump of concrete tied to it.

The scene suddenly came into my head. There's me, sat at a table, surrounded by whiskery old aunties telling me how I should run my life, with the gorgeous Jade Labardia actually SERVING me, as if she was my servant. How gobsmackingly, hideously, revoltingly, sick-makingly, serially sad.

'She said she thinks it'll be quite a laugh,' he persists.

'With me as the star turn, no doubt . . . Brilliant, I can't wait.'

'I'll ask her to slip you an extra piece of cake if you want,' he adds, giggling at my situation.

I chuck one of the rubber rats that litter the floor at his head but luckily see the funny side before looking around for something heavier.

'Talk about *Four Weddings and a Funeral*,' I say, 'I'd rather go to a dozen funerals than this poxy load of poo-dom.'

'Yeah, funerals are cool – much better than weddings. I'm getting a hearse when I can drive.'

'Oh sure, why not get half a dozen?'

'No, seriously, I've heard you can pick them up for practically nothing second-hand. For some reason nobody seems to want them. Mum and Dad think it's a great idea. Did I ever show you that movie *Harold and Maude*?'

'Yes, you spazoid. I lent it to *you*, remember?'

'. . . this rich kid has a big thing about faking his own death and hangs around funerals all the time.'

'Yeah, I know – I lent it to you, remember?'

'. . . and his mum buys him an E-Type Jag which he turns into a hearse and he gets off with this really wrinkly old bird – talk about cool?'

I worry about Merlin sometimes.

'Just imagine,' I say with a laugh, 'me turning up at my house in a hearse, wearing dreads and with an eighty-year-old girlfriend. I reckon my parents would drop dead on the spot and *I'd* have to drive them to the bloody crematorium in it.'

'Oh, your mum and dad are all right. Just a bit straight, I reckon. You're lucky! Imagine having parents that frighten children and animals in the street.'

Much as Merlin's embarrassed by his off-the-planet parents, I need a lot of convincing. At least they don't want him to be a Quantity Surveyor or wear a flipping dark grey suit.

He opens his laptop and clicks on a document called *La Maison Doom*. This is the working title for our new movie, which we are co-producing and directing. Merlin is going to be the male lead and his two sisters are to be the co-stars. The plot's a bit gory, but don't blame me – it's mostly Merlin the Maniac's idea.

LA MAISON DOOM
Produced and Directed by Joe Derby
and Merlin Labardia

Two beautiful French sisters, Mireille and Francine (played by Sky and Jade), are orphans and live in a big house in Paris. Their mother (played by Merlin's mum) had been driven to suicide by their cruel father (played by Merlin's dad). He was a taxidermist (animal stuffer to you) and had treated her practically as a slave.

For years the two girls had watched how their dad had stuffed all his animals and had even been allowed to do small stuff (ha ha!) themselves – like mice, sparrows and the odd baby (only joking!).

Les deux mademoiselles de Paris decide to murder their dad and stuff him to teach him a lesson for what he did to their mum. They find the recipe for a brilliant poison made from stinging nettles, which makes him go mad and froth at the mouth (we put that in purely for effect) *while killing him.*

(Can you see my dad agreeing to do that?)

Anyway, Sky and Jade – sorry, Mireille and Francine – make a wonderful job of stuffing their ex-dad. (Merlin and I reckon we can make this bit look dead real by operating on a large leg of pork and pulling out stuff like liver and kidneys. Pigs' skin is a bit on the thick side, unfortunately, but it'll have to do. Sorry – back to the plot . . .)

The two girls put their surprisingly natural-looking ex-papa, who's now back in his clothes, in the window of his workroom, so that passers-by can still see him behind the net curtains. (We reckon they might have to jiggle him about a bit now and again, to avoid suspicion.)

All goes well, until a young policeman (played by Merlin) *notices that their father's old car, parked in a back street, is not taxed and pays the girls a visit. The beautiful girls, who obviously don't get out much, fancy the young man* (even though it is Merlin) *and seduce him. Unfortunately for him, they're still on their quest to wreak vengeance on the whole of the mankind –*

. . . that's as far as we've got.

Merlin looks a bit worried.

'Look, I think you might have to be the cop. You can't have me doing it with my own sisters.'

'They aren't your sisters in the film. Anyway, you don't mind doing it with mine.'

'Yeah, but we're not related. Anyway, I thought you fancied them.'

'Yeah, but I don't think I could do a full-blown sex scene with them – even if it is pretend – not in front of you, anyway.'

Merlin ponders for a second. 'Maybe they could just lead you off into the bedroom and sort of wink back at the camera – you know, like they do in *Carry On* films. Then we could leave the rest to the imagination.'

'What, both of them at the same time?'

'Look, Mr Superstud, we've only got an hour for this film, you'll have to get on with it. We haven't got time for you to have them separately.'

I must admit I can think of worse ways of spending the odd hour than being dragged off to the bedroom by the Labardia sisters for a rampant sex session, even if it isn't going to actually happen. Come to think of it, the idea might just enter their gorgeous heads some time later. I agree to do it.

Merlin again. 'I reckon the next scene should have the girls back operating on the old pork again – but this time it's you that's being stuffed.'

I'm just about to say there's an awful lot of stuffing going on in this movie, but think better of it. They are his sisters after all.

'What do you reckon they should do with me when I'm done?' I ask.

We sit back a while for a big think.

I suddenly have a brainwave. 'I've got it. The two girls set the dining-table and place me next to their father at the head. Then, as they continue to seduce and murder every guy that comes to the house looking for the one before, they gradually fill up all the chairs. It ends up like a full-blown dinner party of stiffs. We can use some of the blokes from school.'

'Like a macabre meeting of the Masons, sort of thing. Wicked or what!'

'Yeah. The only one to leave the table would be their dad, who Jade and Sky would have to put back in the window every now and again.'

'It'll be like *American Psycho* except we keep all the bodies in one piece.'

We work on for the rest of the morning, defining and refining the plot. At around one, Merlin's mum phones Merlin on the house intercom and calls us downstairs for something to eat.

'How's the film going, you two?' she asks.

How weird it is to be taken seriously by a grown-up. She's so bloody cool.

Scene 5

*The mysterious and fabulous Kingdom of Joe Derby
(my bedroom). 10.00 a.m. on the day of the wedding.*

ACTION:

Honestly, you'd think World War Three had broken out outside my room. It's Saturday morning and there's three whole hours to go before Zoe joins herself in Holy Misery to Graham. I try to get back to sleep, but it's no use – it's like trying to kip in the backstage changing-rooms of a frantic fashion show. Even Rover's crept under the blankets to get some peace. I reckon he hates weddings as much as I do.

'Where's my tights?'

'How long are you going to be in the bathroom? I'm bursting.'

'Have you seen the hairdryer?'

'Where's those knickers with the lovebirds on – the ones I bought specially?'

I stumble downstairs to breakfast.

Oh *merde*, it's my Great-Uncle Harry sitting at the kitchen table. I try to go into instant reverse – you know, like they do in 'Tom and Jerry', but it's too late, he's seen me.

'Ah, Joseph, and how are you this fine morning? All ready for your sister's big day? My, how you've grown. Just think, in no time at all it'll be you walking up the aisle to wedded bliss – ha ha!'

I grunt something just to register that I'm sharing air space with the old fart and try to get to the Sugar Puffs. My Great-Uncle Harry, Dad's uncle, a life-long bachelor (much to my deepest suspicion) is just about the heartiest person you could ever hope to . . . *avoid*. A pillar of his local church, scout leader (hmm!) choirmaster (double hmm!), town councillor and goodness knows what else, he treats everyone in the same way – men, women, children and pets. By talking to us all as if we're not only deaf, but also brain cell-free retards, he continually reminds us of what a superior being he is . . . not.

'I expect you'll be sorry to see your sister leave, won't you, young man?'

'I haven't real–'

'Well, life goes on, I always say,' he says (always), 'you never get anywhere if you don't move on, don't you think?'

I attempt a weak reply to his ludicrous statement of the bloody obvious, but am bowled aside like a wobbly skittle at a bowling alley.

'I never went down the old marriage road myself, as you well know, Joseph. I'm afraid Miss Right never came along.'

'Or *Mr* Right?' I mutter under my breath.

'Beg your pardon?'

'I missed the flight,' I answer, hoping he won't pick me up on it. Luckily the old fart only transmits and hardly ever receives.

'Are you walking out with a young lady at the moment, lad?'

I try to reply, 'I don't really h–'

'Plenty of time for all that, I expect you think. Quite right. Couldn't agree more. Now's the time for your studies and getting a good solid career under your belt. Oh yes, plenty of time for all that other malarky later. What line do you think you might go into, my boy?'

'I'm only in year ten . . .'

I mouth the next bit along with him – 'Well, my boy, you could do far worse than think about local government like yours truly (he means himself). You'll never be a millionaire, I'll admit, but you'll always have security, a good steady living and be able to hold your head high in any company.'

. . . and I'll always be a boring, self-opinionated, red-faced old tosser like you, I so wished I had the guts to say.

Zo flies into the kitchen looking like Miss Haversham in *Great Expectations*. She was the scary old bird that'd been dumped at the altar when a young woman, and decided never to take her wedding dress off – ever. (Mind you, if Graham dumped Zoe it would be the best thing that ever happened to her.)

Zo, who's already put on her dress, has put her hair in curlers and slapped thick white foundation all over her face.

'Oh my God. This is a complete and utter disaster. I can't find my eyelash curlers anywhere. Have you seen them, Joseph?'

'Sorry, Zo – last time I used them was Tuesday. I've just joined that new transvestites' club – the one down in the High Street. It's very n–'

'Well, where are they, then?' she moans distractedly. She obviously hasn't heard a word I'd said.

'Why don't you ask Uncle Harry if he's seen them?' I add, fairly sure the old twerp won't get the innuendo.

'I'm sure she'll look perfectly radiant, curled eyelashes or otherwise,' he says in his most smarmy, chocolaty voice, but by this time the whirlwind that was Zoe has flown out of the room again.

Mother comes in, looking about a hundred.

'Joseph, what do you think you're doing lounging around? It's nearly time to leave for the church.'

'Blimey, Mother, churches aren't like airports. You don't have to be there two hours before for check-in. Why don't you sit down like a good mummy and have a cup of tea?'

'I'll give you cup of tea. I've got your father upstairs on his hands and knees searching for his cufflinks; Zoe in floods of tears saying she can't go through with the wedding because she can't curl her eyelashes; Graham's just rang to say his dad's just fallen off the attic ladder, trying to find his top hat, and sprained his wrist . . . and you look like you're going to a rave rather than your sister's wedding.'

I ought to explain. I refuse to wear anything in bed apart from my *Alien* T-shirt – the one with the alien in question bursting out of my blood-splattered chest – it's really wicked. So was the film.

'Never been late for anything in my life. Not me. Forward planning, that's my motto now and always has been. Oh yes, plan ahead and you'll never go far wrong, you mark my words.' Great-Uncle Harry, looking more self-important than ever, flicks an imaginary speck of dust off his spotless top hat, which is sitting smugly on the kitchen table.

Poor Mum, realising the comment was obviously meant for her, makes wild stabbing movements behind his back. She's always hated the old bugger's guts, but has always been too polite to tell him to his face.

Zo flies into the room again.

'Oh my God, where's my garter? I can't get married without a garter. It's tradition.'

I really can't see the point of weddings. I've only been to two but that's quite enough, thank you. Why can't two people just shack up together if they feel like it without going through all that palaver? I bet my dad would agree. He's having to shell out pocketfuls of dosh for the damn thing.

And what are garters all about? I reckon they're so

that brides can lift up their big skirts to reveal a bit of leg for the photographers – just so that, when they're old, they'll have something to cackle over. 'Ooh, Zoe, weren't you a one when you were young!'

If I ever get married (which I won't) it'll be somewhere really cool like Barbados or Columbia, and all I'll do is send postcards to all the people who should have been invited, wishing they *weren't* there. Unless, that is, I'm marrying one (or both) of the Lambardia sisters – then I'd want everyone to be there.

It's now half-past twelve and the white Rolls Royce is outside. Mum's all done up in a dreadful powder-blue suit that makes her look like the Queen Mother and poor Dad has at last managed to squeeze into the same morning suit that he wore for his own wedding – anything to save money, poor bloke. As for me, I feel like the proverbial spare prick at the wedding – new suit, white button-down shirt, shiny tie and sensible shoes. At least I managed to find a pair of black shades in the hope that I might at least look a bit like Will Smith in *Men in Black* (even if I'm not black).

Suddenly Zoe appears in full kit at the top of the stairs, wearing that pathetic little-girl-lost-in-a-big-cruel-world expression perfected by Lady Di on her wedding day. Mum bursts into floods of tears, causing rivulets of black mascara to run down her freshly powdered face and Dad bites his lip so as not to appear a wuss in front of us men.

At this point, if this was a film and I was directing it, I'd have Zo trip over Rover, who'd be asleep on the top step, only to end in a mountain of organza and satin and suffocating Great-Uncle Harry who's waiting at the bottom to greet her.

Sorry – back to the real world.

Old Harry, puffed up as ever, strides forward and takes Zo's arm just as if my father isn't capable, which he probably isn't. Poor old Dad, hardly able to move due to the tight suit, waddles after them towards the waiting car. I've never been in a Roller before, and it looks like I'm not going to now. The rest of us – including the various aunties, uncles and cousins who've been turning up during the morning – have to go in those horrible Sixties Daimlers that smell like the insides of old ladies' handbags.

'Fine motor-car the Daimler,' says Great-Uncle Harry. 'Just listen to that engine.'

'I can't hear nothing,' I say gloomily.

'Exactly, my boy. British engineering at its best, that's what that is – none of your Japanese rubbish. We could still teach those little . . .'

Talking of old ladies (which I was), why is it whenever there's a wedding, gangs of 'em suddenly appear from nowhere like *Gremlins*? All along the route, the pavements seem to be lined with old dears saying things like 'Aaah! Doesn't she look lovely? Do you remember when our Ethel married Sidney?'

By the time we get to the church, the old lady contingent has increased to near crowd proportions and I have to practically beat my way through the silver-haired rabble to get inside. I feel like the star of a senior citizens' rock concert.

We're met at the door by some of Graham's plebby mates playing at being ushers. Ushers are the blokes who are supposed to separate the two families into different sides – a bit like rival teams at a football match.

I dive for the back row.

'Oh no you don't,' says Mum in a loud stage whisper. She grabs my arm and attempts to frog-march me up to the front while curtseying to the altar (where God lives) and saying hello to a complete set of my ghastly rellies, all whispering about me at the tops of *their* voices like I'm invisible.

'My how he's grown!' – 'Quite the young man, isn't he?' – 'Doesn't he look like his Uncle Cyril!' – and so on and so on. I'm not too wild about being an Uncle Cyril look-alike. He was the one caught exposing himself to a troupe of nuns in a park in Luton. Actually, what is a collection of nuns called? And another thing, why *do* people whisper in church? I thought God could hear everything anyway.

In the front row, on the other side, sits Graham, looking like he's about to pee himself with nerves. Next to him is what I work out must be his best man.

Blimey, there's less clear skin on his face than spots – he looks like one of those join-the-dot puzzles. If he's the *best* Graham can rustle up, heaven help the rest.

Mum again. 'Don't you know you shouldn't wear sunglasses in God's house – it's wicked?'

All the great-aunties nod approvingly, telling her that you've always got to keep an eye on lads of my age. This muttering builds to a small roar until everyone in the church orders everyone else to shush. The old dear on the wheezy organ leaps into the air and plunges into what I presume must be the wedding march:

>Daa-daa-de-daaa,
>Daa-daa-de-daaa.
>Daa-daa-de-dee-daa
>De-dee-daa-de-daaa.

This is the signal for the whole congregation to turn round (except me) and go 'Aaaah!' at the bride.

Here, at last, comes our Zo (well, I think it's Zo) smothered from head to foot in layers of peach-coloured nonsense with my dad, practically crippled by his too-tight suit, struggling to keep up. As she gets near the front, the gross porkster that is Graham, turns round and leers at her in the most disgusting I'm-going-to-have-you-tonight sort of manner. If I was Zo, I'd be belting out of the church as fast and as far as I could – like the girl in *The Graduate* (except she had Dustin Hoffman waiting for her). What *was* her name?

The rest goes mainly to plan. Zo lisps her way through all the 'I dos', 'I promises' and the 'I'll never do it with anyone else till we're dead' routine, until the bored vicar, sounding like he's just done fifty of these things before lunch, tells them that they're now man and wife.

The shiny new Mr and Mrs Bunt emerge triumphant in all their sickly glory from signing some certificate thingy that now says they're married, and prepare to stroll back down the church, nodding and smiling to everyone. The old organ grinder, obviously anxious to get back for her afternoon nap, crashes into that song they always use for walking out of church at far too fast a gallop, causing the happy couple to practically jog down the aisle. Poor old Zo, having left the confused bridesmaids way behind, has to hold her own skirt up to avoid going flat on her newly-wed face.

As soon as we're outside, I turn round to see if there's anything good in the girlie department. Nothing doing, as usual, apart from one of the bridesmaids who looks fairly tidy but who, I suddenly remember, is a first cousin which means, according to Mum, I can't go near – 'because you get stupid babies'.

As I'm wondering if it's worth the risk, a skinny girl with glasses and braces on her teeth, runs over.

'You don't remember me, do you, Joseph?'

'Er, sorry I – um . . . Are you one of my Luton

cousins?' I say, feeling sure I've never clapped eyes on her in my life.

'No, silly, I'm Graham's younger sister. You met me on New Year's Eve. Don't you remember? We went into your dad's shed. I'm Gay.'

I feel pretty gay for not remembering and keeping out of her way.

'Graham's sister?' I say, as it all floods back. Hell, I never realised she was Graham's sister. 'How are you doing? I thought you might be here,' I lie, not very well.

'Wasn't it a lovely wedding? Doesn't your sister look lovely?'

'Lovely,' I murmur distractedly.

It was coming back thick and fast. This bird Gay's about the same age as me. She was the one that cornered me on New Year's Eve at Mum and Dad's weedy party. I was fed up from the start because the Labardias were having a real rave-up that ended up going on all night. I was made to stay at home with my own grown-ups and their friends.

I did manage to get stuck into a couple of lagers, however, and by midnight this Gay girl was beginning to look almost passable. I must have been a bit pissed or I would never have gone near her. Especially if I'd known she was Graham's sister. This news makes it even worse.

Anyway, just as everyone was about to do that stupid dance where they hold hands in a circle and dash in and out ('Old Lang's Iron' or something) we went out to Dad's shed and snogged a bit. I remember because I can still recall the metallic taste in my mouth – like sucking a bunch of keys. She then started getting a bit carried away and began putting her hands all over me. I remember so clearly now. I started to get a bit tight in the trouser department, much against my better judgement, but just as I was about to put my hand down *her* front, I heard someone coming out into the garden.

I was saved by my own father, as it happened. He'd slipped out for a sneaky illegal fag but, thank God, he'd taken them out of the shed earlier. Anyway, it was just enough to cool things down and once he'd gone I managed to manhandle her back to the party.

'So, are you going to the reception?' I ask, looking her over properly again. Actually she looks better than I remember. Quite tall for a girl, with long, slightly motley legs. A bit skinny, as I said, but then so's Kate Moss and I wouldn't kick her out of bed. She's got blonde hair – natural, I think, and dead straight. To be honest, she looks as if she might be somewhat lacking in the breast department, so I probably wouldn't have had much of a result had I gone any further in the shed that night.

At last I have time to take in all the guests and it's not a pretty sight. Practically everyone coming out of the church looks as though they've logged on to

UnsuitableClothesRUs.com. Why do women with fat legs wear short skirts and great big hats? It makes them look like toadstools. And why do they make little boys wear shirts with collars that they could get two of their scrawny little necks into? And why do they put little girls in those awful frilly socks with slightly high-heeled shoes? And why do men wear grey shoes? There's never been an occasion in the history of the whole wide world where you could get away with grey shoes – ever!

By this time the photographer's practically foaming at the mouth.

'Could we have the bride and groom with her parents – the bride and groom with his parents – the bride's family – the groom's family – the bride and groom kissing (urgh!) – the bridesmaids – the bride chucking her posy to the bridesmaids – the bridesmaids giggling – the best man and ushers – the best man and ushers with Zoe showing her garter – all guests with bald heads – all guests with wooden legs – all the smokers – all the drunks – all the transvestites – all the junkies – you name it.'

I managed to duck behind the group I was in, making pretty sure there's no record that can ever be used in evidence against me. Now it's back in the car and off to the Great Northbridge Hotel for the bit I'm dreading most.

Scene 6

The Great Northbridge Hotel.
Saturday 3.00 p.m.

<small>Warning! This could get a bit gruesome.</small>

ACTION:

The Great Northbridge Hotel is one of those huge pubs like you see round all big cities. They're usually covered in stick-on wooden beams to make them look Tudor, but aren't. Allow me to give you a guided tour as we stroll through its famous portals. Pause for best BBC voice.

We wedding guests, having walked through the historic oak-panelled lobby (built around 1950) complete with suits of armour (also 1950), pass the Henry VIII Carvery – 'all you can eat for all you can spend', and the Napoleon Brasserie – 'Northbridge's answer to Paris'. We then have to follow the signs up the stairs to the Nell Gwyn Suite. Boy, do I love historic buildings.

Mum and Dad and Zoe and Graham and his mum and dad – the Bunts – are lined up at the entrance and everyone's supposed to shake their hands as they go in.

No way, José! Not me. You won't catch me shaking hands with anyone – let alone the new Mr and Mrs Bunt.

I turn round and search for the gents' to have a swift pee and work out my next move. I can either hang around here until everyone's gone in, or try to sneak in without anyone seeing. I peek round the door. Luckily, I catch sight of my huge Auntie Hilda rolling towards the Nell Gwyn Suite like a galleon in a heavy sea. I dive in behind her and stay safely in her wake until she reaches the welcome committee. I then vere off to one side and into the main room. I've hardly gone two metres when I get a nudge in the back.

'Would your Lordship care for a drink? Champagne, Bucks Fizz or methylated spirits.'

I whip round and see it's Jade, Merlin's sister, carrying a tray of drinks and looking more fantabuloso than ever.

'Hiya, Jade, how's it going? I bet you never thought you'd see me done up like this. Gross, isn't it?'

'I hardly recognised you. You look about ten years older. It's weird but that suit really suits you – honest.'

'If that's a joke, it's in pretty poor taste, thank you ever so much.'

'Seriously, Joe, you look dead cool.'

I can see that she's looking at me strangely – up and down – almost as if she's never really seen me before.

'Look, I can't talk now,' she says, 'I've got to work, but try and cheer up, it might not be as bad as it looks. Anyway, I'd better go. 'Bye – er – sir.'

Jesus Christ, I can hardly think straight as she walks away with a dead sexy wiggle just for me. She's wearing a short black skirt, black tights and a white shirt that you can almost see through – wow! I don't know what it is about uniforms, but I reckon she looks better than any of the female guests by about eighty times. Mind you, that's not saying much. I look down. Damn, I've taken an orange juice by mistake. That's girls for you.

Making sure I'm out of sight of Mum and Dad, I grab a proper drink off another waitress and start watching the families Derby and Bunt meeting for the first time.

Mum, still red-eyed from crying because she's happy (eh?), is chatting to a funny little man in a kilt who I suppose must be a Scottish Bunt (or would that be a McBunt?).

'Aye, they're a fine couple to be sure, Mrs Derby,' I overhear. 'She'll make him a fine wife, I'll be bound. I was only saying to Morag this . . .' Why are there always men in kilts at weddings?

Dad's talking to Mrs Bunt, Graham's mum, who seems to have favoured a floaty pink marquee and has topped it with a ridiculous white hat that looks like and is about as stupid and useless as the Millennium Dome.

She says, 'Me and Mr Bunt always thought, from the moment we met your Zoe, that we'd be hearing the tinkle of wedding bells. I wouldn't mind betting that in another nine months we might just . . .'

. . . might just still be waiting for Graham to learn how to do it properly, I think to myself.

Old Great-Uncle Harry, standing right in the middle of the room, thumbs in lapels, is talking to, or rather *at*, Mr Spotty the best man.

'Mark my words, young fellow, you can do far worse than consider a career in local government. You might not ever be a millionaire but . . .'

Zoe seems to be huddled with the bridesmaids. I wonder if she's discussing what she might get up to tonight, after lights out. The newly married Graham seems to be swallowing champagne like it's going out of fashion.

A huge voice right next to me makes me almost spill my drink.

'LADIES AND GENTLEMEN – PRAY BE SEATED FOR THE WEDDING BREAKFAST.'

God knows why they call it a breakfast, it's nearly teatime.

A much smaller voice comes from the other side. 'Hello, Joseph, glad I've found you again. Guess what? You're sitting next to me – isn't that a coincidence!'

Oh heck, it's the Bunt girl again. Coincidence, my arse! I bet she's switched the table thingies.

'I think we'd better sit down,' she says, grabbing my arm and dragging me through the hoards of manic guests scrambling for their tables as if they've just announced a ban on all food starting in ten minutes.

Oh no, I'm on the same table as Great-Uncle Harry.

'Well, I must say, your father's done us proud, young man. This will have set him back a pretty penny, I'll be bound,' he chortles, unbuttoning his waistcoat in preparation for all the free food he's going to shovel down his fat gob at my dad's expense.

I catch my poor dad sitting sad and alone at the top table, looking as if he's only just realised that this lot are going to chomp through the best part of his pension.

'I eat so little these days,' says the mournful Auntie Hilda, who's already polished off three of the bread rolls from the middle of the table and is holding her knife and fork at the ready.

'Have they got chips, Mam?' asks Brian, my cousin, who's just finished picking his nose. Brian fell off a swing when little and has never been quite the same since.

'Not today, dear, we're having proper food. Now sit quietly and stop doing that with your fork.'

'I don't believe I know you, my dear,' bellows Great-Uncle Harry to a rather mousy-looking lady sitting next to him.

'I'm Doreen, Graham's mum, Mr Bunt's first wife. I don't think they really wanted me here, but I had to see my boy getting married.'

Gay looks at her in astonishment. Blimey, perhaps she doesn't know she's got a different mother to

Graham. I'd have danced round the room in pure joy! Great-Uncle Harry looks almost lost for words. Nobody seemed to know Graham's dad had been married twice. We assumed the old pink marquee was Graham's mum – she's certainly fat enough (I reckon I should call her Mrs 'Bunter' from now on). Old Harry can't stop himself, however, and ploughs ahead regardless.

'Never you mind, my dear, you're welcome at my table,' – note the '*my* table' – 'whatever anyone else thinks. Did he leave you long ago?'

The little woman suddenly looks well put out.

'Leave *me*! I left him. She was the third woman he'd messed around with since we were married.'

She points to Mrs Bunt the second, sitting next to Dad on the top table. 'She can have him for all I care, she couldn't wait to get her hands on him.'

We have prawn cocktails to start with. Auntie Hilda takes hers at a gallop and eats it in two ginormous mouthfuls before nicking poor Brian's, saying, 'Oh well, if it's going begging.'

I've never known a prawn cocktail to beg for anything, but I don't make a thing of it.

Great-Uncle Harry, having finished his first, proceeds to tell us how prawns only eat the crap off the bottom of the sea and that it's that which gives them their flavour. Gay Bunt just giggles and says that she always thought prawn cocktails were drinks.

Just as we're finishing lunch, the bloke in the red

jacket with the loud voice, yells out: 'LADIES AND
GENTLEMEN! PRAY SILENCE FOR THE BRIDE'S FATHER.'

Dad, looking totally miserable, stands, clears his
throat and does the usual thing, thanking everyone
for coming and hoping they'll have a good time.

'I'm sure I – er – speak for Barbara, in saying that
we couldn't have handed Zoe over to safer hands.'

Safer than who? I ask myself. Hannibal bloody
Lector?

'Finally, I'd like to hand you over to the best man,
Nigel, who I'm sure has a few – er – impromptu
reminiscences about his best friend and my new – um
– son-in-law.'

Weedy applause.

Oh, God, here we go again. I shuffle down in my
seat and wish the world would end.

Mr Spotty gets to his feet, reaches for his inside
pocket and takes out his few 'impromptu'
reminiscences.

If I slip any further down my chair, I'll be under
the table.

He proceeds to tell this ghastly story about an
occasion when him and Graham were at the church
youth club. Graham had bet him a pound that he
could touch the breasts of all the girls in the room
without them even noticing. He'd apparently cruised
round the church hall brushing against all the girls,
taking pieces of imaginary fluff off their cardigans, or
pretending to look more closely at the youth club

badges pinned to their chests. Just then, the vicar and his young wife came in.

By now everybody at the reception, including the waitresses, is deathly silent and a slight quaver starts to come into Mr Spotty's voice as he realises he hasn't really got the audience with him.

'The vicar's wife,' he continues, 'was rather well-endowed bosom-wise and, believing that nature and gravity should take their course, had lately taken to wearing a rather thin T-shirt saying *Jesus Saves* – with no brassiere underneath.' A few people in the audience thought he meant *Jesus Saves With No Brassiere Underneath* and tittered out loud.

The aunties are now craning forward in disbelief, trying to catch his every word. Graham has turned scarlet and is looking pleadingly at who is rapidly turning into his *worst* man.

'Out of the blue,' he continues, 'a large wasp landed on the vicar's wife's right breast. Our Graham, seeing his chance, leaped forward and smacked it hard with the palm of his hand and crushed it. The wasp stung the nearest thing to it and the poor woman leaped into the air, crying for someone to get an ambulance. It turned out she was severely allergic to wasp stings and that she'd die if she didn't have an anti-histamine injection right away.'

Total silence.

As soon as the ambulance had taken the poor woman, now in a coma, to hospital, Graham had come running over to him with a big grin on his face and asked him for the pound.

'You really should have been there,' Spotty said miserably. 'It was so funny.'

Total silence.

Just as he's about to continue, Mr Bunt leaps up, thanks him, edges him out of the way and asks Graham if he'd like to say a few words. Graham, now streaming with sweat, stands up slightly shakily and addresses the stunned guests.

'Nigel's such a laugh, isn't he, ladies and gentlemen. The things he comes out with.' He turns and glares at his ex-best friend like he could shove a bayonet right up his backside.

'Anyway, enough about me. First I'd like to toast my beautiful bride's wonderful parents for giving us such a wonderful day and having such a wonderful daughter.' He reaches below the table and hands my mum an expensive bouquet that, no doubt, my poor dad had shelled out for. He prattles on for what seems hours.

'. . . and lastly I'd like to toast *my* parents for being so supportive.' He then turns round and hands the pink marquee another bouquet equal in size to my mum's.

At this point the little woman on our table turns to the rest of us and says far too loudly, 'She's not his mother, I am. If it weren't for me he wouldn't even be here.'

She then bursts into tears and runs from the room.

I really can't stand much more of this, my embarrassment quota is practically used up – and we've still got the cutting of the cake. I tell my shell-shocked table companions that I need the loo and sneak off. Luckily everyone is far too distracted by the weeping woman to even notice me.

I find a small door saying Fire Escape at the far end of the Nell Gwyn Suite and slip out into the fresh air. Blow me if Jade isn't sitting on the metal stairs smoking. We look at each other for a split second and then both fall about laughing.

'This is the best wedding I've ever been to by a milllion,' she says, tears running down her face. 'That best man's speech was the biz. What a div. Why did Graham choose him?'

'Probably the only friend he's got. Sorry, the only ex-friend he's got.'

'And that woman running out crying. You couldn't have got better if you'd paid her. Talk about an Embarrassogram. Who was she?'

'Graham's real mum. I think he must have had her on *his* list – silly fool.'

Suddenly, out of the blue, Jade pulls me towards her and kisses me full on the lips, pushing her tongue between my teeth and deep into my mouth. I nearly collapse with shock. Things like this don't actually happen in real life.

'I've been wanting to do that all afternoon, Joe,'

she says in a really sexy voice. 'You look so cool in those clothes. I've only seen you as Merlin's little friend before this.'

I dive back before she changes her mind and kiss her beautiful lips until I almost faint with excitement and shock. My head whirls and loads of little lights seem to go off in my brain. Her long hair smells exotic, a bit like the joss-sticks Merlin burns in his room. I swear I will never forget that smell as long as I live. She holds my hot face between her cool hands and looks into my eyes long and searchingly until I have to look away. I feel so young – so inexperienced – so bloody little.

'You really are very beautiful,' she murmurs, running her slim finger round my mouth. 'I could just eat you alive.'

Eat me! Eat me! Just don't bloody stop, I say to myself, completely out of my depth.

We kiss again and this time I put my tongue right into her mouth. She tastes just like she looks – sweet and delicious and only slightly cigaretty. It feels so intimate, almost rude – blimey, what must it be like to go the whole way? After a few more minutes we pull back for air and she lights another ciggie. Suddenly the fire door opens and there's Gay. Luckily she's peering round the other way, so by the time she spots us we're a good metre apart.

'Ah, there you are, Joseph, I've come to find you – the dancing's starting.'

'Oh, hi . . . er . . . Gay, this is . . . er . . . Jade, she's an . . . um . . . old school friend of mine.' Luckily Jade's a lipstick-free zone, otherwise it would give the game away. Hang on a mo! What am I saying? I *want* to give the bloody game away. I *want* to tell everyone. I'd like to go back in that room, walk up to the top table, bang it hard and shout, 'Look you lot, I've just kissed probably the best-looking girl in the world!'

'You go and dance, Joe,' says Jade with a sly twinkle, 'I've got to go and help clear up.' With that she gets up and slides past Gay who doesn't appear to have noticed a thing. Talk about beauty and the beast.

The Victoria Ballroom.
Saturday 7.00 p.m.

ACTION:

Quite honestly, Gay Bunt could lead me to the nearest window and chuck me out of it for all I care. Is this what being in love's like? Do you always float four metres above the ground feeling like a right zombie? It's spooky, it's just as if Jade's still here. I can still hear her soft, sexy voice ringing in my ears, her joss-sticky smell is still right up my nose, and I can still feel her wonderful breasts pressing against me (whoops! I nearly said mine!).

She kissed me – ME! She really kissed ME. I didn't have to do a bloody thing, did I? I didn't know girls ever did that sort of thing. I simply walked out on to the fire escape and Jade kissed me full on the mouth and with tongues involved. What did she say? She'd been wanting to do it all afternoon. WOW! Wanting to snog ME all afternoon. Jade Labardia, Merlin's gorgeous sister, *wanting* to snog me, ordinary old Joe Derby, all afternoon.

I look round and I appear to be in the Victoria Ballroom. I suppose I must have walked with Gay all the way down the stairs and through the lobby without noticing a thing. Zoe and Graham are in the middle of the floor dancing alone with one of those goofy revolving balls right above them chucking beams of light, like you see in prisoner of war movies, into the surrounding throng.

'The bride and groom always start the dancing at weddings like this,' says Gay. 'Don't they look lovely.'

I presume she doesn't require an answer and if she does, she isn't going to get one. I look over towards the band. Five guys with awful mullet haircuts (they could even be wigs) are playing some soppy love song that I almost recognise. It reminds me of the band in the opening scene in that fab film *The Commitments* – the one made by Alan Parker about a bunch of kids starting a soul band in Ireland. At the moment there's the usual double-bass, piano, saxophone and drums line-up plus, of course, the singer. That's bad enough but, tucked behind them, I can spot a cluster of electric guitars and keyboards which, *without* any luck, they'll get out later for us 'young' people.

Great-Uncle Harry invites the Pink Marquee to accompany him in the waltz – pompous prat. This is the signal for all the grown-ups to sail round the floor like awful old dodgem cars, banging into each other and running down any kids who get in their way.

I don't really do dancing – far too tribal for me – but proper dancing gets the saddest of the sad prize. Almost sadder, I notice there's not enough men to go round so most of the old ladies have to make do with each other. Tragic or what?

I suddenly feel like I want to chuck up. This 'being in love' business sure plays havoc with your guts, especially when you've had a few drinks. Turning my back on Gay, I rush to the nearest gents, find a cubicle, then say a fond farewell to my personal wedding breakfast – prawn cocktail and all. When I've flushed the loo and shoved some water in my face, I go back to the cubicle, close the door, lower the seat and sit down to have a proper think.

I wonder what she's doing now? (Jade – not Gay.) I wonder if she's sitting somewhere thinking about me? After all, it was her that had the problem all afternoon. Hang on, Joey boy! Don't start to get too cocky. Half an hour ago you didn't even know *she* knew you really existed. For all you know she's snogging someone else on that very fire escape right now.

I tear out of the loo, across the ballroom, up the stairs three at a time, sprint across the deserted Nell Gwyn Suite and out on to the fire escape. Thank God, there's no one there – all the afternoon staff appear to have gone home.

I sit down on the same step where it all happened and put my head in my hands. I wonder if she'll tell her sister about me? Jesus, what will Merlin say? I must tell Merlin. If only I had a mobile. Oh no, if I had a mobile I'd be trying to ring Jade and that would break all international uncool records. I mustn't speak to her until she contacts me. I really mustn't.

Or should I? Aren't men supposed to take the lead these days? Isn't that what women like best? You can bet Brad Pitt didn't wait for Jennifer Aniston to make the first move. Oh God, but the last thing I want is to make a dick of myself.

Hang on a minute, I suddenly realise that the Joe Derby she actually said she fancied wasn't me but the bloke in the suit. What's she going to think when she sees me again in the old skater's gear I usually wear? I'll be just like Cinderella, turning back into Merlin's 'little' friend again. I'd also be like that guy in the movie *Cyrano de Bergerac*, except I'm the *same* bloke – the ugly one *and* the good-looking one. But I can't go around wearing a suit all my life, my mates will think I've lost the plot completely. This is so weird. I've just snogged Jade Labardia and I'm feeling totally fed up?

'Ah, there you are, I've found you again. What are you doing sitting out here all on your own?'

I turn round quickly, hoping against hope it's Jade, but know full well it's got to be Gay Bunt again.

'Oh, sorry,' I lie, 'I suddenly felt like I was about to throw up and came up here for a bit of fresh air.'

'They've nearly finished the old-fashioned dancing, it's time for our music.'

Your bloody music, maybe, I say to myself. That lot would have a blue fit if they played my sort of music. I can just see Auntie Hilda and Great-Uncle Harry waltzing to Fear Factory or Machine Head.

'C'mon, Joseph (I hate people calling me Joseph), don't be a spoilsport, come and dance.'

'The Mullet Brothers' have taken off their blazers in favour of seriously sad sparkly bomber jackets, worn with shoestring ties and dark glasses. They're now well stuck into a sad medley of Seventies hits, all played at exactly the same pace and in exactly the same key.

I have to giggle to myself, watching the oldsters dancing to what they think is young people's music. It's so sad. And they think they're so good at it. Worse than that are all the little kids, who should be in bed (or tied up). Especially the little girls, who've obviously seen the Spice Girls or some equally gruesome girl band on telly, going through all the boob-thrusting, bum-waggling movements, not having a clue what they're all about, while their parents look on proudly. It's all a real gross-out. Beam me up, Scotty as they say in 'Star Trek'. Please beam me up!

The band is now having a go at a load of Rolling Stones hits and the singer thinks he's amusing everyone with just about the worst impression of Mick Jagger ever – clapping his hands, sticking out his stupid fat lips and wiggling his bottom. I think it's safe to say the Stones can all sleep peacefully in their old people's homes – the Mullets of Northbridge aren't about to replace them this week.

I go through the motions of dancing but I don't really give a toss whether I look cool or not – Jade's gone and that's all that matters. Jesus, it all comes back to me again.

Was it true? Did I really snog Jade? Tell me I'm not imagining it.

The head Mullet now speaks in a fake American accent: 'And now, for all you late-night lovers, we'd like to slow the pace right down. Here's our very special version of "Strangers in the Night".'

Oh shit, it's the smoochy bit where the drunkest people *reeeally* embarrass themselves. I'm still sort of with Gay, it appears, and without any hesitation she lunges at me, throws her arms round my neck, shoves her tongue down my throat and grinds her bony hips into mine. Oh no, not again. Not 'Miss Metal Fatigue' again.

'Do you remember New Year's Eve?' she coos. 'You got a little excited, didn't you?' I think she means IT got a little excited, but I don't pursue it.

'I can't really remember, I think I was a bit pisse–'

'We were in your dad's shed,' she persists.

Really, I almost say, I thought it was a satellite going round Venus . . .

'We could go upstairs to your little secret place outside if you want.'

The idea of sitting on that sacred step with Gay, after the astonishing Jade, fills me with horror. Oh no, she's nibbling my ear now, and her hand's going on safari into the deep south. How the hell am I going to get out of this?

Suddenly 'Strangers in the Night' turns into 'Stranglers in the Night'. An argument has broken out on the other side of the dance floor. Zoe is having a go at one of her bridesmaids who she's caught chatting up her brand new husband.

Graham, now pretty drunk, is lurching about, trying to make out he knows nothing about it. Luckily Mum and Dad have already gone, so they won't have to witness the imminent scrap. Tee-hee, it looks like lover-boy might not be getting his wicked way with my sister after all tonight. What a waste of the Cleopatra Bridal Suite.

As all the girls, including Gay, try to quieten things down, I creep out of the hotel and begin the long walk home. I told Mum and Dad that I'd be getting a lift with Great-Uncle Harry, but I need to be alone. Before I even realise, I find myself going on a long detour, which involves passing – you've guessed – the Labardia house. I don't even know why.

It's past midnight and they're probably all in bed. I realise quite soon, as the odd motorist slows down to peer at me, that I'm swaying a bit. The demon alcohol strikes again. After about half an hour, I get to Chestnut Drive and the Labardias' massive house, looking more like the Bates Motel than ever in the moonlight. I'm pretty sure Jade's room is at the top on the left. I feel a bit like Steve Martin in *Roxanne* but there's nothing to climb up and I don't do poetry. Not that I would if I could.

I don't believe it! The light's still on. I sit on the wall on the other side of the road and try to imagine her up there, just like Romeo in Baz Luhman's *Romeo and Juliet*. I wonder if she sleeps with anything on? It's a warm, muggy night and I can almost see her stretched out on her bed, naked apart from a slight smile, staring at the ceiling, thinking of me. I should be so lucky. I try to will her to come to the window.

I read once in one of Zo's daft magazines that if you really concentrate hard on someone's mind you can actually get through to them. I don't usually believe all that stuff but anything's worth a try. I close my eyes and try to think of her beautiful face till it almost hurts. 'Please come to the window, please come to the window, please come to the window,' I say over and over until I actually start to wonder if I'm getting through.

Suddenly the sash window opens. Blimey, it's worked. I might have to start believing in all that stuff!

Unfortunately it's Merlin's dad, Tony, trying to let some air into the room – I've got the wrong bloody window.

I stroll home feeling really gutted. I thought being in love was supposed to be the best thing ever. I feel

worse now than before this whole thing happened –
far worse!

Scene 8

The Kingdom of Joe (again).
Sunday 11.30 a.m.

ACTION:

It's Sunday morning. My head feels as if it's being squeezed in one of those car crushers and my mouth tastes like I've been licking the inside of Rover's bowl (or worse). As my sad brain gradually begins to stir, I suddenly remember I'm in love with Jade Labardia – the gorgeous, sexy Jade Labardia. I try to picture her face, but can't quite get it – bad brain alert! I can almost, but can't quite bring it into sharp focus. I need a photo . . . I so need a photograph of the girl I love. I jump out of bed only to realise my brain's come loose overnight and is banging against the inside of my skull. Rover, who must have crept into my room when I came in, regards me with a look of superior disgust.

'Please, God, don't let me die yet, I'll believe in you for ever – honest.'

I lower myself gingerly back on to the bed and check the time. Blimey, I must have slept for . . . er . . . I can't work it out. A hell of a long time, anyway.

I've got to ring Merlin, but I can't use the phone downstairs, they'll *all* listen. By all, I suddenly remember it's now just Mum and Dad. Hey, I wonder if Zo took her mobile? Maybe not. I don't suppose the new Bunts wanted to be disturbed in the Cleopatra Bridal Suite – that's if they even slept together in the same room after last night. I must admit the idea of Graham doing it to my sister nearly makes me want to rush out to decorate the toilet bowl again. Mind you, to be fair, I always feel the same about my mum and dad.

I creep unsteadily to Zoe's room, a right mission in my state. Luckily she always did leave the door open even when she was walking about with nothing on. It used to intrigue me, I'll admit, when I was a little kid (no willie and all that) but when I got older it made me feel kinda queasy. It's funny, you'd go through anything to catch a peek at any another girl's rude bits, but your sister's or your mother's (or your Auntie Hilda's) are a real turn-off. Yippee! Her phone's still on her bedside table and it doesn't need a code. Back in my domain I dial Merlin's special number. The Labardias have got this special switchboard thingy in their house that means they can each have their own phone. Flash or what!

'Hi, Merlin, how you doing?' I croak.

'Great – I've just written another bit of the film. Listen, you know when they've got all the stiffs sitting round the . . .'

I can't get into all that now, so talk right over him.

'I just wondered if you ran into Jade this morning?'

'Jade? Yeah, in the kitchen. Why? Why do you wanna know? You sound dreadful.'

'Did she mention anything about the wedding?'

'Yeah, it sounds like a riot. What a hoot, man! How did it all end up? She said she left just as it was getting interesting.'

'What was getting interesting?'

'What? What do you mean WHAT? The wedding, you div, what do you think I mean?'

'Did she mention seeing me?' God this is hard work.

'Yeah, she said you looked cool in your suit. I said I couldn't believe it. You in a suit – no way.'

'Did she say anything else?'

'Like what? She just said she was tired and was going back to bed. Why?'

I feel like I'm in Richard Branson's hot air balloon that's suddenly popped and flopped into the sea. Surely she'd have mentioned her and me becoming *friendly* at least! Blimey, she said she'd been wanting to snog me all bloody afternoon. Oh hell, if only I could just see her again.

'Are you all right? You sound awful.' It was Merlin, still on the phone.

'Er, sorry, er, yeah, I'm all right, sort of. Look, can I come round? I've got something I've got to talk about or I'll burst.'

'What – now?'

'Yeah, I'll be there in as long as it takes – see you.'

I put down the phone and start throwing clothes on. Suddenly I stop dead. Hang on, Joey boy, you know full well you're not *really* going round there to see Merlin. You know all you want is to casually bump into Jade – accidentally on purpose. But you can't go dressed like this. She won't even *notice* you in your usual clobber. I can't wear the suit either, it'll look daft on a Sunday morning – like those blokes that come to your house selling God or The Salvation Army, or something.

I sit on the bed in near panic. What the hell am I going to wear? Just about everything I've got, apart from school clothes, has got holes in or is covered in slogans. Skate-wear's all right for mucking about in, but it ain't exactly a great bird-puller. Hang on, I've suddenly got a brainwave. My dad's not much bigger than me, perhaps I can find something in his wardrobe.

I see the funny side just in time. Headline:

SHOCK HORROR! STYLE GURU JOE DERBY
RAIDS DAD'S WARDROBE FOR SOMETHING
GROOVY TO WEAR!

That's as bad as Prince William breaking into the old Charlie's dressing-room to find something for a rave.

Let's think again. Perhaps it was all that dark stuff that turned her on. Come to think of it, both Jade and Sky always wear a lot of black. Hang on, I could wear the nearly-black suit trousers with that black sweater

I got last Christmas from Gran. I look out of the window. Damn and blast! A cloudless sky. Why would anyone be wearing a heavy sweater in the middle of a scorching summer, you cretin? What about a T-shirt? I know I've got just about every colour under the sun . . . but nothing black. Not in one piece, anyway.

Wait a minute, didn't Zoe once wear a black T-shirt thingy when she was mooning round the house in mourning after she'd broken up with Graham for the umpteenth time? I dive back into her room and go straight to her wardrobe.

Luckily Zo's always been really girlie about clothes so everything she's ever owned is stored in poly bags on hangers. Sure enough the black T-shirt's there and looking like it's never been worn.

It must be my lucky week for getting clothes to fit. I look at myself in the mirror. Not bad, my son! Black T-shirt, nearly-black trousers, black shoes and, oh yes, the black sunglasses still in my suit jacket pocket. Forget wedding outfits, this really *does* look cool. The only thing wrong is that I smell a bit of Zoe. I slap on a bit of Dad's aftershave to try to hide it but that makes it worse.

Mum and Dad are in the dining-room as I tiptoe downstairs and try to escape without them noticing.

'Ah, there you are, Joseph, we thought you'd died. Mind you, you do look a bit ghostly.'

'Give us a break, Dad, it **is** the day after your beloved daughter's wedding.'

'We didn't hear you come in. Were you very late? You look very smart again, where are you off to? And where did you get that top?' asks Mum with her puzzled face on.

'Which question do you want me to answer first, *mon capitaine*? I suppose I have come in the right door for the Spanish Inquisition?'

'I spoke to your Auntie Hilda this morning. She said you were getting on very well with Graham's sister last night,' Mum continued with a little wink at Dad.

'She was getting on very well with *me* more like. I had nothing to do with it. Now can I go?'

'When you've had your breakfast. You always have a cooked breakfast on a Sunday.'

'Sorry, Mum, but I really don't think I could even keep down a bacon sandwich. I think I must have eaten something that didn't agree with me.'

Dad looked up from his paper. 'Oh, so it had nothing to do with all the booze you managed to get your mittens on, I suppose.'

It goes backwards and forwards like Wimbledon for about ten minutes before we both accept a draw and I finally break away.

Scene 9

The Labardia house.
Sunday midday

ACTION:

I get round to Merlin's house, ring the doorbell, close my eyes and pray for Jade to answer it. The door opens.

'Hi, Joe, got over yesterday?' It's Sky – worse luck. I wonder if she knows about Jade and me. Is that what she means by 'got over'?

'Hiya. Yeah, just about. Still a bit delicate, though. Is Merlin in?'

'Yup. Go on up. He's in the Hammer House of Horrors.'

I notice she's looking at me strangely too, but put it down to my new look.

I walk slowly up the stairs, making as much noise as possible, hoping Jade just might hear me and come rushing out of her room. But I reach the entrance to Merlin's gloomy domain with no such luck.

Merlin opens his door and stares at me.

'Blimey, it's the Cadbury's Milk Tray man. I think you've got the wrong door, mate, I don't much like chocolate or my men in black. What's that funny smell? Have you turned into a home-owner overnight?' ('Home-owners' are what we call gays, by the way.)

'I borrowed Zoe's top, it pongs a bit of her perfume. C'mon, let me in.'

'A bit! You'd better be careful or I might start fancying you. Crikey, you smell like a Turkish brothel. Don't let anyone else meet you stinking like that.'

That's all I need. Now I've got something else to worry about.

'Want a cuppa? The kettle's just boiled.'

'Yeah, that would be great. I've got a mouth like the bottom of a gerbil's cage. Never will I drink the demon alcohol again, may the Lord be my witness.'

Merlin returns from the dark recesses of his kitchen with two black mugs. 'Now, what's the big prob? Something about last night? Did you disgrace yourself – I hope?'

'I thought Jade might have told you.'

'Told me what?'

'About us?'

'Us what? Look, what are you going on about?'

'Oh, just that we snogged at the wedding on the fire escape.'

'Oh *that*. She mentioned *that* this morning.'

'She did? Why didn't you tell me?'

'Tell you? I thought you'd know. You usually know when you've snogged someone.'

'OK, smart arse, what'd she say?' I'm getting cross.

'Erm . . . nothing really.'

'Her exact words . . . please?'

'Oh blimey, let me think. She told me about the

best man's brilliant speech, then she said she went out the back for a smoke and that you came out and had a bit of a snog.'

Somehow this sounded worse than her not mentioning it at all. At least, before, she could have been so embarrassed about the way she felt that she couldn't mention it to anyone close. This just sounded as if it was about as important as the fag. I suppose it lasted about the same amount of time, come to think of it.

'I think I'm in love with her, Merlin. I can't get her off my mind. I feel sick all the time.'

'LOVE? What, with our Jade? You sure? Jeeesus, that's a new one. LOVE?. . . Does she know?'

'Well, I suppose she'd know if she feels like me,' I say feebly.

'Wow, man, sorry I was so crap. I don't know what love feels like. I know how it feels when you want to tear someone's clothes off and drool all over their body, I used to be like that about your sister. But *love* – I haven't a clue what that's all about. I hope it's not catching.'

'I thought it was only something in girls' mags and soppy films, but I never thought it hurt. Honest, Merlin, it really hurts. I sat outside your house for ages last night – just hurting.'

'My house? What time? After the wedding?'

'Yeah, it must have been around twelve thirty.'

'What are you going to do? Are you going to tell her?'

'I would if I really thought she felt even a bit like that about me. But I could make a right prat of myself if she doesn't.'

'I wouldn't tell her smelling of someone else, even if it is your sister – that'd really put her off.'

'But how can I find out without asking?' This is all getting worse.

'I could ask Sky. They tell each other everything.'

'Would you?'

'Sure, I can't have my best mate mooning about like a lost llama. Look, I'm not sure when. They're going out somewhere today. If she *is* really into you she'll spill the beans then.'

'Thanks, mate, I owe you one. By the way, don't let Sky know I'm in love with Jade, just ask as if you're really nosy, as if you suspect something's going on but don't know for sure.'

I feel slightly better, until I start thinking that the two sisters are probably out with their *real* boyfriends at this moment. Insecure, *moi*?

'By the way,' I add, 'you haven't got a picture of her, have you?'

'Oh sure, I always carry a few piccies of my sisters on me. Sorry, mate, I mustn't joke. Look, I could take a couple of stills off the test we did for the film. I can put it through the computer and print them out. Blimey, you have got it bad.'

I should add at this point that Merlin's got just about every bit of kit it's possible to have – from computers to hi-fi to video. I can't complain, though, he lets me borrow most of it whenever I want.

'Can we do it fairly soon?' I say, trying to appear not too urgent.

'Oh, all right. It'll take a little time, I've got to put it on disc first.' Merlin goes over to the computer for ten minutes.

It's dead funny, I must have seen that bit of video a hundred times but never just looking for Jade.

'Where do you want me to stop? There's a bit with her laughing here, see.'

'No, go on, there's another section where the girls are trying to look sexy, you know, when the detective comes in. Can we stop there?'

We get to a part of the film where the camera goes right in on Jade's face and she looks directly at the camera. It's exactly the expression she used when she looked at me yesterday. Oh hell, I feel so wrecked.

'There! Stop there! Sorry, Merlin, could you stop at that bit, please, mate?'

Home again.
Sunday 4.30 p.m.

ACTION:

When I get home, clutching Jade under my T-shirt, I find Mum and Dad have just got back from collecting the wedding photos – the ones they took yesterday. They'd taken them to that three-hour photo place in the High Street first thing this morning. Aren't grown-ups funny? They spend the best part of a whole day with people they haven't seen or thought about for yonks and then, only a day later, can't wait to look at them again. Still, who am I to talk? I can't seem to be able to live much longer without pictures of a certain someone I *have* seen practically every day for a couple of *years*.

It's no good, I can't get out of sitting down with them to look at the snaps. Poor old Ma and Pa, I suppose it's all they've got to show for the small fortune they must have shelled out.

'Isn't that a good one of you, Derek? You could almost be mistaken for the man I married,' says Mum with a little giggle.

Dad replies grumpily, 'I wish I still was the man you married – I might fit that blooming suit a bit better.'

Next pic.

Mum again. 'Auntie Hilda's a wonder now she's had her hip done. Isn't she a size, though?'

'For someone who reckons she hardly eats,' I chip in quietly.

Next pic.

'Ooh, isn't that the woman who ran out of the room crying? Who invited her? She wasn't on our list, was she?'

'I suppose it must've been Graham, someone said she's his real mother. I bet he regrets it now – miserable old bag!'

'Really, Derek. You can be so unkind. Imagine how you'd feel if your daughter was getting married and you hadn't been invited.'

'A damn sight better off, for starters,' said Dad mournfully, still smarting from the expense of it all.

They thumb through the pictures a couple of times and then something suddenly dawns on Mum.

'Joseph, I can't see you in any of these. Where were you? It's such a shame, all that money spent on a new suit and there's nothing to show for it.'

Oh yes there is, I say to myself, holding my precious pictures close to my chest.

'It was a lovely day, though,' she continues dreamily. 'We were so lucky with the weather. Zoe and Graham looked ever so happy.'

That's before the fat slug was caught chatting up one of the bridesmaids, I nearly say – but don't. It reminded me of that really funny American film called *The Heartbreak Kid*, where this really uncool bloke gets chatted up by a very young Cybill Shepherd on the first day of his honeymoon and then tries to get rid of his wife. Mind you, it *was* Cybill Shepherd – not some dorky old bridesmaid.

I eventually manage to break free and crawl up the stairs to my room. I suppose I really should eat – I haven't touched anything since I was sick yesterday. Mum said they're having Sunday lunch at teatime today and that it'll be ready in half an hour, but I'm not really hungry. Funny that – Mum usually has to run around like she's got the human equivalent of a cuckoo in the house, shovelling food down my throat just to keep me alive. Perhaps what they say about not being hungry when you're in love is true. I'd better get over it soon or I'll waste away.

I go through the pictures that Merlin printed out for me with Rover, but he doesn't seem that impressed. Honestly, if Jade was a *real* movie star she couldn't look any better. But why does it hurt so much when I look at them? I put the pictures away, but her face is now everywhere – even Rover reminds me of her. Something about the eyes. I need to talk about it so badly, but how can you talk to anyone who's not in the same boat? How could anyone else know how you feel? Bugger, bugger, bugger!!

It's weird – yesterday morning I was just an ordinary, five-out-of-ten-happy bloke, going to his boring sister's boring wedding in a boring suit. Now

I'm suicidal and will soon be dead from malnutrition, all because I met a girl I really fancied who seemed to really fancy me.

I just have to know what she's thinking. For all I know she's in her room at this very moment, feeling just the same (if you believe that you'll believe anything, Joey boy). Will Merlin ring as soon as he's spoken to Sky? Perhaps Jade's so annoyed at having snogged me, that she doesn't want to talk about it. No, that can't be right, otherwise she wouldn't have mentioned it to Merlin, even if it was in the same sentence as having a fag.

I go down to supper when Mum calls and sit quietly at the table.

'Are you all right, dear?' she asks in a soft, mumsy sort of voice. 'Your dad and I are a bit worried about you – you don't seem your old self.'

I suddenly feel like bursting into tears and telling her everything – but not Dad. He'd say, 'You shouldn't be worrying about girls at your age,' or something equally crap. Having said that, there are some things even your mother can't help you with.

'Too much drink if you ask me,' said Dad, who wouldn't spot an emotional crisis if it hit him on the back of his bald head.

'You're probably right, Dad,' I say quietly, not even bothering to come back with a smart remark.

That fact alone made both of them look at me even closer.

'You're not mooning over the young Bunt girl, are you? Don't say we're going to have another Bunt in the family?'

THAT'S IT! As Popeye used to say, '*I can't stands no more.*'

'Oh, shut up, Dad!' I shout. 'Why don't you just leave me alone? I don't give you a hard time every time you're a bit pissed off!'

I rush out of the dining-room, just managing to hold back the tears, and dash up the stairs to the only place where I feel safe. Rover follows me up, knowing I might need him.

So this is what being in love's like, is it? I think I'll stick to lust in future, it's much safer.

The Kingdom of Joe.
Monday 7.30 a.m.

ACTION:

I hardly sleep a wink on the Sunday night, thinking about Jade. This has to be the very lowest point in my life, and just to make it even lower, I have to go back to school in the morning. I sometimes think that criminals must feel like this when the old judge tells them they're going back inside again, except the food's much better, so I've heard. Life really sucks!

The only good thing about going back this morning, as far as I'm concerned, is that I might run into HER. The drag is, HER is a year ahead of me and usually no decent girl from that year would dare to be seen having anything to do with us Year Tens (or Year Elevens, as we will be from now on). We usually just watch them walk by, tongues hanging out (ours not theirs), discussing which ones we'd give one to. All us guys yap continually about who we'd deign to sleep with and 99.9 per cent of us never have. Funny that.

Merlin's late as usual, so I can't grill him about what has gone on between Sky and Jade. All through assembly I keep searching his face for some sign that it might be good news.

Our school's supposed to be quite good according to people who've never been there, but isn't that like most things. We've got a fairly new head teacher, Nigel Bowen-Smith (we call him Lord Nige) who, as you might have guessed from his name, would really prefer to be running some posh public school rather than some two-bit suburban state set-up like ours. If he had his way, we reckon, there wouldn't be any girls at all and we'd all be going around in poncy outfits with naff straw hats like they do at Harrow or Eton.

'I say, Derby minor, would you be so kind as not to run in the corridors, there's a good fellow, but do come round to my rooms later for tea and crumpets.'

We've never been too sure which side Lord Nige bats for, on the old girlie front, but we're pretty sure there isn't a Mrs Bowen-Smith – and he does walk a bit funny.

We belonged to last year's infamous 10C, which is now 11C. If the teachers had their way we'd all be in the D-stream but that's strictly for pond-life. Kids from the D-stream usually turn out to be soldiers, policemen or traffic wardens. We heard from someone that traditionally all new teachers are given us lot to start with, as a sort of trial by fire. I think it goes along the lines that if they can teach us, they can teach anyone – a bit like putting the circus chimp trainer in with the lions – sort of sink or swim (or eat or be eaten). It makes us feel kind of proud, in a way.

Not much has happened to my classmates over the summer. Slim Jones reckons he went all the way with that Donna Brightwell from Year Eleven in the park shelter, but said she wasn't much cop. We didn't believe him and anyway Merlin reckons anyone would be 'quite considerable cop' if they went all the way.

Treadwell's father, who's a chiropodist, took him and the rest of his family to the Caribbean, where Treadwell trod *badly* on one of those black spiney things you get in the sea out there and was unable to walk for the rest of the holiday. Funny, I thought feet were what chiropodists were good at.

Browning, who thinks he's dead smart, tried to drive his dad's new four-wheel drive while they were staying on this farm in Devon, and practically wrote it off when he ran into a cow. The cow, apparently, came off all right, which says more about Japanese pretend Land-Rovers than anything else.

Best of all by far, was 'Dickie' Davies's dad, who ran off with the school's lollipop lady, according to Spike Adams. Poor old Davies had to put up with licking and sucking jokes all day. Ha, ha!

The first period on the first day is double History. Our teacher, Peter 'The Fly' Philips, is ready and waiting and looking meaner and meatier than ever. He got his name because Merlin reckons he once auditioned for the film *The Fly* – not for Jeff Goldblum's part as the mad scientist . . . but the fly. He didn't get it because he wasn't big enough. Anyway, he's looking extra hunky and freckly following his fortnight in Margate in his elderly mother's caravan. (I think we made that up, but it's funny, so who cares?)

We are supposed to have done a whole load of stuff on the Romans over the summer but neither me or Merlin even opened the books. I planned to do it yesterday but all I could think about was Jade. Anyway, I thought I'd get away by going to see the fantabuloso *Gladiator* a couple of times but am now not too sure how accurate it really was. I really must have a word with Ridley Scott, the director, over drinks one evening.

Philips The Fly hits on me straight away.

'So let's start with Derby, our resident historian. Mr Derby, pray tell, who was the first Roman general to visit Britain in 55 B.C. and what did he find when he got here?'

I'm miles away, imagining what Jade's doing at this precise moment. I wonder if she's thinking about me?

'Erm . . . Could I phone a friend, sir?'

'Ooh, please, sir, I know.' It's Baker, head creep from Creepland-on-Sea, waving his stunted little arm around, trying to catch teacher's attention.

'In a minute, Baker, I'm sure Mr Derby is just organising his thoughts so that he can give us a half-hour presentation on pre-Roman Britain.'

'Well, sir, it's quite difficult to know exactly what they were up to,' I say, stalling for time.

'And why is that, pray tell?' he says in his supercilious I-may-be-weedy-but-I'm-cleverer-than-you voice.

'Um, well, we Ancient Brits didn't know how to write until the Romans came,' I guess, 'so there can't be that many history books to tell us.'

Philips looks a bit taken aback, but not as aback as me. It wasn't the answer he was after – it was actually better. Jade would be proud of me!

'Er, well, yes, that is probably true,' he says grumpily. 'The Romans did bring writing to Britain. Ah! But you haven't said who was the first to invade. What about your colleague Mr Labardia? I'm sure he's been swotting up all through the holidays. Labardia, please enlighten us as to who was the first Roman general to lead an expeditionary force to our shores. Surely you should know – aren't you half-Italian?'

'Yes, sir, but my grandad came over a bit later.'

Thank God for that, I think to myself, otherwise there'd be no Jade (or Merlin, come to that).

Merlin obviously knows no more than I do, but Spike Adams, the official class clown (and our other best mate), whispers something that I can't quite catch.

Merlin obviously does. 'Was it Nero, sir?'

'Many thanks to our History don, professor Merlin Labardia, for his inspired answer. No, it wasn't Nero, I'm afraid he was rather busy being emperor back in Rome at the time.'

If Baker's hand goes any higher it'll come out of its socket and flap round the room. 'Baker, tell him who it was.'

'Julius Caesar, sir,' the smug little bastard answers, grinning all over his rotten little face.

I'm fairly sure that Julius Caesar was played by Sid James in *Carry on Cleo*, but reckon that information might be surplus to requirements.

'Right, and what legacy did the Romans leave us?'

Merlin whispers to me, 'This is turning into the 'What did the Romans Ever do for Us?' sketch in *The Life of Brian*.'

Baker pipes up again. 'Legionnaires' disease, sir.'

'No, you stupid boy, that came from the American Legion, a group of US army war veterans. It's *roads*, for heaven's sake.'

At this the whole class breaks into an uproar of cheers and jeers and all those around Baker dig him with whatever comes to hand.

I hardly register what's going on. I just can't wait to get Merlin on his own to find out about Jade. Five minutes to go till break.

'The Romans were the first to build proper roads throughout Britain. How would you recognise a Roman road now?'

Baker *again*. 'Would it be falling to bits, sir?'

'No, you dimwit, Roman roads were built in straight lines for mile after mile, probably because there was no enclosed land to skirt round.'

'How did they know where they were going, sir?' asks Spike innocently, but The Fly realises he's taking the piss and ignores him.

At breaktime Merlin and I get a couple of Cokes from the machine and walk round behind the gym where he rolls a ciggie.

'Well, did you speak to Sky?' I ask, almost before we sit down. 'Did she say anything to Jade?'

'Look mate, I'm sorry, but I'm not sure you're going to want to hear this.'

'Hear what? What did she say?'

'She said that she spoke to her last night. Jade thinks you're very cute but . . .'

'Cute? Did she actually use the word "cute"? What total pants! Puppies and kittens are cute, for Christ's sake.'

'Look, don't blame me, I'm only telling you what she told *me*.'

'Sorry, carry on.'

'She said that she was in a devilish sort of mood, and you just sort of turned up.'

'Turned up? She said that she'd been wanting to snog me all afternoon. What a cow.'

'Hang on a minute, she is my sister.'

'Oh hell, sorry, mate, I just can't help it.' This really isn't going very well at all.

'She said she's sort of got a boyfriend and she felt a bit bad about what she did. She told Sky she didn't want to lead you on. Look, I'm sorry too, mate. As I said, I'm only telling you what Sky said.'

'Brilliant. I'm so glad I asked.'

'She *did* say that she thought you looked really cool and that in a couple of years' time she'd probably fancy you big-time.'

'Oh, yeah, and by then she'll be after twenty-five-year-olds. Probably the only time I'll stand any chance is when she's about sixty and then I'll probably be too bloody old to even be a toy boy. Anyway, I'm not really sure I can wait that long – even for her.'

'The best thing is that Sky swears that she didn't let on to Jade that you're crazy about her. At least you won't feel stupid.'

Stupidly enough that makes me feel a lot better. At least I can try and grab back a bit of cool from the situation. But who am I kidding? Only yesterday I thought I just might have snatched one of the very best babes around for my very own girlfriend and now zilch – dumped before it's even bloody started. Talk about *Snoggus Deprivus*! Having said that, it's a good job I haven't told anyone either. That could feature rather heavily in the egg-on-face department.

But how should I treat Jade when I see her again? I'm afraid there's only one way. She doesn't know that I know what she said, unless Sky's telling porkies, so I should act as if that snog means as much to me as it obviously does to her – like nothing.

'Kiss? What kiss? At the wedding, you say. Oh, that one, I think I remember. Which one were you?'

Meanwhile, I've got to try to get over it. It's odd, but as I walk back towards school, I do feel slightly better than before, when I knew bugger all about how she felt. Funny that.

Scene 12

Northbridge High School.
Tuesday 9.00 a.m.

ACTION:

If trying to get out of games ever became an international sport, Merlin and I, *Les Deux Slobbonis*, would be off to the Olympics. We obviously can't actually say that we've forgotten our games kit, because:

a) we've done it a billion times before, and

b) that would be lying, and the good Lord says one must never lie. We learned that in RE. Actually, that's a lie – we never learn anything in RE. The truth is, we'd be sent back home to get it.

Most of sport's a load of balls, we reckon. Small ones, big ones, heavy ones, light ones and even oblong ones. Then there's athletics. What, in the name of sanity, is the point of athletics? Throwing things like spears, discuses (disci?) or big heavy balls as far as you can, jumping as high as you can, jumping as far as you can or – more daft still – hopping-skipping-*and*-jumping as far as you can. All this stuff is a mystery to me *and* my mate Merlin. Anyway, we're going to be famous film makers so our time's far too valuable for all that nonsense. Anyway, how can I think about sport when my mind's taken up with Merlin's sister?

It's the autumn term now, however, so we've got to tell old 'Ollie' Read the games master which we want to do – football or rugby. Both involve far too much running about and – worse – getting dirty and having to take showers and stuff – thank you, Mr Read, but no thank you.

Merlin and I reluctantly choose football because, if you *do* have to play, we reckon you can usually stand about for ages talking and not having to do anything until the ball comes your way. Last year Merlin even managed a sneaky fag while it was up the other end.

Merlin thinks for a second. 'I *was* going to put "flower arranging". Do you think old Ollie will go for that?'

'You'd do better to put "detention". That's what you'll end up with.'

My mind drifts off to Jade again. I bet she looks sensational, jumping up and down in a T-shirt and shorts. I wonder what sort of bra she wears for sport?

We eventually crack the problem by telling Ollie that both our fathers aren't working at the moment so can't afford to buy us new boots. We've already told him we'd grown out of the last lot. Poor old Mr Read who, to be fair, will never be called on by the rocket science department, isn't sure he believes us.

'Is this strictly true, Labardia? You wouldn't be lying to me, would you?'

'No, sir,' says Merlin, 'my dad hasn't had a proper job in weeks.'

This is almost true. Merlin's dad, rich though he is, hasn't had a proper job ever.

'And you, Derby. Hasn't your father been working either?'

'No, sir, but he's hoping to go back soon.'

True again. I think he went back today – he's been off for two weeks' holiday. Honesty is always the best policy, I always say.

'Well then, they won't mind my writing to them just to confirm this.'

Could this be a problem? We think not. Merlin's sure his father, who also hated school (and therefore never went), would be cool and say anything he's asked, and my dad's so mean that he'd cut his cheque-signing arm off rather than shell out any more of his hard-earned dosh, especially after that poxy wedding.

Unfortunately old Ollie informs us there was a special sort of 'poor fund', left by some rich 'old boy' do-gooder, to pay for essential equipment for under-privileged kids (that's us, folks), but it'll take a week or so to organise (*quelle domage!!!*). Merlin and I look suitably upset because we can't play today and wait until the silly arse jogs off towards the pitch blowing his stupid whistle. We then hurry to our nice warm classroom to get on with the film. I bet Quentin Tarantino doesn't have to go through all this.

'I've been thinking,' I tell Merlin. 'I don't think I'll be able to do the sex scenes with your sisters after all.'

Merlin thinks for a second. 'I thought we'd already decided that it was all going to happen behind closed doors, anyway.'

'Yeah, but I can't even do it there either now.'

'But you won't have to, will you, you plonker? It'll all be in the mind.'

'Yeah, but I can't even go through it in my mind,' I answer, lying through my teeth. (I've actually been doing it with Jade in my mind ever since Saturday.)

'But it isn't going to be in *your* mind, you dumbo, it's in the audience's mind.'

'Why can't *you* do it, then?'

Merlin looks slightly miffed. 'I told you already, because they're my sisters – clot brain. Flipping hell, what if the public found out all three of the stars have got the same parents? There's newspapers queuing up to print stuff like that. You can just see the headlines –

'*TOP MOVIE STAR* (that's me) *IN STEAMY LOVE TRIANGLE WITH OWN SISTERS.*'

'It'd be brilliant publicity,' I say hopefully.

'It'd be the end of my career before it even started, for Christ's sake.'

'A bit like my wild love affair with Jade.'

'Anyway,' he goes on, 'you've got nothing to lose, and let's face it, it might give Jade ideas. That's what you said when we first thought of it, remember.'

'Oh, all right,' I say, 'I'll do it.' The trouble now is that I know that I'll be going through the dress rehearsals (or undress rehearsals) a million times in my head.

After school me, Merlin and Spike Adams catch on to the tail end of a bunch of girls from our year as they're coming out of the school gates.

'What do you reckon to that Naomi Peters, Merlin?' Spike asks, almost loud enough for her to hear.

'I *would*, despite the nose. She looks quite good in ordinary clothes, we saw her in town over the summer. Do you remember, Joe?'

'Yeah! Great legs, shame about the boat race.'

'She could always get *another* nose,' says Spike.

Merlin chips in, 'What'd she want two for? So's she can smell better?'

'No, you spaz, you can have any sort of nose you want these days with plastic surgery – they've even got catalogues.'

'What, called Nose U Like?' I ask.

'Yeah, it's the same with boobs. In America you can choose what sort you want – big, small, round, pointy . . .'

'I'd have real whoppers,' butts in Merlin, and Spike and I laugh.

'I reckon they'd hurt,' says Spike. 'All that silicon bouncing around in front of you.'

'No, it wouldn't, I'd wear a huge bra,' says Merlin, but this time we ignore him. Sometimes he's too weird for anyone.

'What's it like having a sister with big boobs, Merlin? Does Jade ever let you look at them?' Spike asks.

Merlin glances at me and then tries to change the subject, but not very well. He points across the road.

'I reckon Sarah Deakins actually looks better in school uniform, she wears really straight . . .'

But Spike isn't put off that easily.

'Do you reckon Jade'd pose for a magazine, Merlin, for a lot of money?'

Despite how much I'd like to see Jade's body, I can't bear the idea of people like Spike ogling over her.

'Look, you div, why don't you keep your dumb questions to yourself!' I shout. 'If you can't shut your mouth, I'll shut it for you!'

Poor old Spike nearly jumps out of his skin.

'What's up with you, Joe? I only said . . .'

'It's OK, mate,' says Merlin, grabbing his arm. 'It's a bit of a tricky subject.'

'Yeah, well I only said . . .'

I turn to Spike. 'Look, I'll tell you about it sometime, OK?'

'Yeah, well I only . . .'

'Look, you retard, let it go, will you?' I shout, and rush on ahead.

'Yeah, well . . .' I hear him shout after me.

The Kingdom of Joe Derby.
Tuesday 5.30 p.m.

ACTION:

It's the evening and I'm in my room – sort of sulking. I wish I were dead. Well, maybe not actually dead – that's a bit final. What I *really* wish is that I could be a few years older so that I could *really* get off with Jade Labardia. But that's like wishing our rotten school would burn down. Where's that blasted good fairy when you need her most? She did it for Pinocchio and he was just a boring old lump of Italian wood. Rover looks straight into my eyes as if he almost understands, but anything less like a good fairy I've yet to see.

I remember that film, *Summer of '42*, all about guys of my age having their first goes at sex. One lucky kid is dragged off to bed by a real babe of an older woman. Her young husband's just been killed in some war or other and she sleeps with the kid because she's a bit pissed off. She dumps him, of course, when she comes to her senses. I know now exactly how he felt, except I didn't even get to the good bit.

Poor Spike, I really tore into him this afternoon. He couldn't have known what I'd got myself into. I'll tell him I'm sorry tomorrow. It's so stupid, just as I begin to feel a bit better, Jade's blasted face starts invading my head. It's like bloody *Zulu* all over again but this time their new queen, Jade Labardia, seems to be able to stroll in whenever she wants. I can't even look at those pictures Merlin gave me – they're now lurking on top of the wardrobe in my rucksack, almost begging me to get them down. Seriously, I'm beginning to wish the whole thing had never happened – I knew I should never have gone to that damn wedding. It's all Zoe's fault. Thanks to her I'll be embarrassed when I do see Jade again – if I *ever* see her again. I've got to think of something or someone else.

I get out my magazines from under the mattress and look at all my girls again. Charlotte from Cardiff with small boobs and a big cheeky smile; Donna from Doncaster with huge boobs and a tattoo of Robbie Williams on her thigh; Tracy from Exeter with a beautiful . . . well, anyway, I wonder what they're doing at this precise moment? Surely they can't be lounging about in seductive poses all the time? It's funny, I know every inch of their bodies, but I haven't a clue what they're really like as people. I often wonder where they live and whether they show their nudie pictures to people at work or even their mums.

'Ooh, that's an interesting one, dear. How did you get yourself into that position? It looks so uncomfortable,' *or* 'Isn't that *my* nail polish you're wearing? I thought I recognised it,' *or* 'Does the photographer go out of the room while you take your clothes off?' *or* 'You do remind me of your Auntie Doris in that one.'

To tell the truth, I can't even concentrate on *them* at the moment. I keep seeing Jade's head on *their* bodies, which makes it even worse.

I hear the phone ringing downstairs.

Mum calls upstairs. 'Joseph . . . telephone. It's Spike. He says he's got to talk to you.'

'Sorry, Mum, could you say I'm busy? I'll see him tomorrow.'

She calls up again. 'He says it's important. Could you come down?'

I go down.

'Hi, Spike.'

'Hi, Joe. Look, about this afternoon, don't go off on one again, but Merlin told me what happened. Look, I'm really sorry, mate. I bet I'd feel the same if I ever got within a mile of a girl like that.'

'Thanks, Spike. I was going to say sorry, too. It's just that I can't get the stupid bird off my stupid mind.'

'Cor, I don't blame you, she's a serious babe – not in my league at all. I can't believe you actually snogged her. Did you do tongues and everything?'

(I wonder what he means by everything?)

'Look, Spike, don't tell anyone else about all this – I feel such a prat.'

'Prat? You must be barking. You got off with

119

practically the best-looking girl in the universe and you reckon you're a prat? Jesus, I dream of being that kind of prat. What was it like?'

I realise that, despite trying to avoid it, this could actually be the conversation I've been so waiting for. I couldn't talk to Merlin because Jade's his sister and I can't talk to my mum because I'll blub and seem like a kid, but I'll bloody burst if I don't dump on someone and it might as well be Spike.

'Look, what are you doing now? I can't really talk at the moment – *Zulu alert!*' I turn round and see Mum hovering around, trying to look busy. 'Do you want to meet in the park?'

'Sure. What about the shelter? See you there in ten. OK – bye.'

Mum was waiting just by the front door when I'd finished.

'What have you got to tell Spike, dear? What do you feel so stupid about? You can tell me, I'm your mother.'

If her voice hadn't been so kind and soft and all sort of caring, I'd have jumped down her throat for snooping.

'Oh nothing, Mum, I'll tell you about it some day, promise.'

'I've noticed you being a bit quiet lately. Even your father was saying you've been easier to live with.'

'Look, I can't talk about it now, Mum, honest. I've got to go down the park to meet Spike. I said I would.'

Scene 14

The Northbridge Recreation Ground shelter.
Tuesday 6.30 p.m.

ACTION:

Spike's in the shelter adding his name to all the others that claimed to have *had* a rather friendly girl, rather appropriately called Stacy Allcock, who lives over on the council estate. He turns round and looks at me with a something approaching awe.

'So come on, Joe, what was she like?'

'I can't really describe it. It was nothing like ordinary snogging – wondering how far you're going to get and all that. It was like kissing a real proper grown-up woman, like in the movies.'

'What, no teeth bashing and noses getting in the way?'

'None of that, she knew exactly what she was doing.'

'And was it *really* all her idea?'

'Yeah, all I did was turn up on the fire escape at this wedding.'

'And you now reckon she doesn't want to see you again?'

'I don't know about not wanting to see me again, I just think she thinks I'm too young.'

'For what?'

'To go out with. She's into much older blokes, according to Merlin.'

'Do you think she goes all the way?'

It's odd. Although I've been all the way with her in my head (and hand!) about a trillion times, I've never really thought about her actually doing it with anyone else. It's too gross for words.

'I suppose most girls of sixteen have,' I say mournfully.

'Would you have if she'd let you?'

'Course,' I say, without thinking.

'Did you have the necessary equipment?'

I nearly say 'of course' again, but then realise there are some conversations where, if you don't tell the truth, there's no point having them.

'No, I – er – didn't.'

'Hey, what if you've got it wrong? What if she really does fancy you?'

'Sky told Merlin that Jade said she was just having a bit of a laugh.'

'Yeah, but she *would* say that, wouldn't she? She's hardly going to tell her big sister she fancies a bloke a year or so younger than her. Honest, if she's snogged you once, she won't mind doing it again. You've just got to play it cool. I'm really useless at cool, but I reckon you could do it big-time.'

Before I realise, I'm actually giving dear old Spike a hug. He's made me feel so much better.

Just then Tracy Turner, Laura Jacobs and this new girl called Lucy something walk past.

'Well, well, if it isn't Joe and Spike,' says Tracy.

'Sorry, boys, we didn't realise you two were an item. Well, we'll let you carry on in peace. Your secret's safe with us.'

'Very funny,' says Spike. 'It just happens we're meeting some girls here later, if it does actually happen to have anything to do with you.'

'Have you got time for a quickie with us first?' Laura giggles.

Even in the early evening light I can see that Lucy, the third one, has gone bright red at her friends' rude talk.

Tracy, the one that spoke first, is also in Year Eleven and lives a couple of streets away from me. She's pretty fit in a Shazzer kind of way – seven out of ten on a good day – but no one in their right mind goes near her because her two big brothers are in a gang, and her dad's apparently been in the nick for grievous bodily harm. Laura, her mate, is a bit plump, with enormous boobs and what could be the beginnings of a small moustache. She follows Tracy everywhere – like those white birds that ride on rhinoceroses' backs – and acts as if she's just as sexy (not as a rhinoceros's back – as Tracy).

Merlin and I have worked out that good-looking girls often have not-very-good-looking mates, either to make them look even better (like parking a Ferrari next to a Skoda) or simply to tell all their much better exploits to.

Lucy, the third one, has only just come to our area

from somewhere like Cheltenham, and seems very shy. She's one of those girls, I reckon, that if she ever managed to sort her hair out and get the right kit on, could hit the dizzy heights of eight or nine. But she always hangs behind the others, and never seems to have anything to say for herself. Someone really ought to do a number on her like in that film *My Fair Lady*. That's the one where Rex Harrison takes the dead pretty but common Audrey Hepburn from the gutter, tarts her up a bit, teaches her how to speak proper, and then introduces her to all his rich mates. He does it to prove the point that you don't have to have been born rich to be posh. Total rubbish, of course.

Laura says, 'Look, we're having a barbecue on Sunday in our back garden. It's my birthday. We've got too many girls. Do you want to come? You can even ask that weirdo Merlin, too, if you want.'

All the girls think Merlin's a bit odd. For a start, he talks to them just like he does blokes – he doesn't know the meaning of shyness or tact. I remember him saying to Laura that if the rest of her was half as good as her tits she'd be gorgeous – to her face, and he once said to Chloe Michaels that she'd be almost all-right looking if she didn't look so pissed off all the time. Loads of stories have got out about strange happenings at the Labardia house, none of which, according to Merlin, ever happened, though most times he wished they had.

I really love that family. I can still remember the

hush during last year's parents' evening when his mum and dad came into the school hall, and how embarrassed Merlin was. His mum was wearing a floor-length velvet sort of caftan with silver sparkly moons all over it and had scarlet hair in braids with different coloured beads, a bit like they used to make poor old Stevie Wonder wear. I reckon you ought to have to have a licence to dress blind people.

Merlin's dad looked a bit like Dr Who, when he was played by Tom Baker, with a cloak, one of those daft floppy hats that hippies wear, and a scarf that trailed along the ground behind him. I suppose, to be honest, I'd be embarrassed as well if my parents turned up like that, but I still think they're great.

Merlin himself gets away with murder at school. He's adapted his school uniform to look like an undertaker's outfit and dyes his hair a different colour practically every few months. If the rest of us were to even try to get away with anything like that we'd be up in front of Lord Nige before you could even say RULES. We all reckon Merlin can do more or less as he likes because his dad offloaded a big wodge of dosh on the school to set up what they now say's the best Art department in the county. Mind you, Merlin *was* told his dreads had to come off immediately he arrived at assembly yesterday morning.

'So, are you going to come?' Tracy asks.

'Yeah, I might,' said Spike, 'if I'm in the country. I should fly down to Monaco this weekend. Staff problems on the yacht, don't you know.'

'Are you coming, Joe?' It's Lucy something. She actually spoke! Blimey. And she's got a really nice, soft voice. I didn't even know she knew my name.

'Er, yes, if it's OK with Laura. Where do you live, Laura?'

'Silverleigh Drive, the road next to Merlin's – number eight. Don't bother bringing anything, my parents will cough up.'

I suppose Laura's folks must be pretty well-off too. The houses in the road next to Merlin's are nearly as big and flash as his.

Scene 15

The Kingdom of Joe.
Sunday 11.30 a.m.

ACTION:

It's Sunday and I really can't work up any real enthusiasm for Laura's barbecue. I know Jade won't be there and I also know that Merlin, Spike and me will probably be the only blokes. It could be all right, I suppose, but usually if you get a whole bunch of girls together they can drive you round the twist. In fact Zululand (our house) is almost bearable now that Zoe and her stupid mates aren't here.

All the same, I put on my new black outfit (I'd managed to sneak Zoe's T-shirt into the wash, so I don't pong of her any more), and with the black shades I reckon I look pretty damn cool – for me, anyway. I ring Merlin to tell him I'll call for him, as he lives in the next street to Laura's.

As I get near the Labardias' house, I stop for a couple of minutes to calm myself down. I haven't seen Jade for over a week, and I have to work out what I'll do if I *do* run into her.

I ring the bell and wait. Three guesses who answers?

'Joe! Hi, sweet.'

It's Jade.

'I haven't seen you since the wedding. How's it going?'

127

Jeez, all I want to do is leap on her, drag her to the ground, smother her in passionate kisses, and say things like 'I've missed you so much,' and 'Can't we just carry on where we left off?' I manage, just in time, to listen to the Angel of Cool who's climbed on to my right shoulder.

'Hi, Jade, yeah I'm good. Is Merlin about?'

Unless I'm completely mistaken, I think I detect a slight puzzled look flicker across her lovely face. Why isn't this kid coming on to me? She's maybe thinking, It's not every day that a lad of that age gets to sample the delights of an older woman.

'Oh – er – yes, I think he's upstairs,' she says hesitantly. 'Do you want a coffee before you go up?'

Lordie, Lordie, she's never offered me that before – ever. The Angel of Cool orders me to play the game right through, however.

'No, thanks. We've got to be at this girl's party round the corner. I'd better go and drag him out of his den.'

Blimey, I'm right. She definitely looks miffed. OK, maybe she doesn't really want me, but it could be well different if it seems like I don't want her either. I don't suppose girls like her have a clue what it's like to be dumped.

'OK, suit yourself,' she says, almost with a flounce, 'I expect I'll catch up with you sometime.'

As I climb the stairs I feel miserable. The Angel of Wimpdom, perched on my other shoulder, would have had me hanging around like a lap dog, drinking coffee with her till the end of time, just for one more little snog, and now I've blown it. I want to rush back downstairs and tell her I'm sorry, that I'm crazy about her and that I've thought about her every second of every minute of every hour of every day since last Saturday. But the moment's passed. What a complete bummer!

Merlin opens the door, without me pulling the bell rope, and catches me staring at the wall.

'Hi, Joe, what have you just said to Jade? She's just rung from downstairs to tell me you're coming up. That's a bit odd for a start. She said you simply haven't got time to talk to her. She sounded really arsy. What'd you say?'

'Look, can I trust you to keep your big gob shut, Merlin? It's all part of a grand plan, you see. Treat 'em mean, keep 'em keen sort of thing. I'm obviously not going to get anywhere by telling her that I love her and can't live without her, but this way I might at least be in with a chance.'

'Blimey, that's a dangerous game. I reckon if I ever tried that, most of the birds I ever try to pull would feel relieved.'

'I don't know how I did it myself. Now I wish I bloody hadn't.'

'Hang on a minute, Joe. I reckon I know my sisters pretty well. They're used to getting pretty much everything they want on the bloke front – it's all just a massive laugh to them. They get through them like loo rolls. I doubt whether either of them has had to go short of guys. I reckon you might have smacked it. Want a cuppa?'

Scene 16

Laura's back garden.
Sunday 2.15 p.m.

ACTION:

I was right – when Merlin and me eventually get round to Laura's place there are girls everywhere, tearing about, whispering in corners, rushing indoors every five minutes to check their make-up and bra straps. What is it about girls? On their own they've hardly got anything to say, but when they get together they turn into a bunch of soppy kids.

Luckily Laura's dad, Mr Jacobs, who's looking totally ridiculous in massive shorts and a chef's hat, hasn't been mean with the beer (my dad would have donated one bottle of shandy and thirty straws). Merlin and I get stuck in right away. Unfortunately it turns out to be that stuff they sell in Sainsbury's which is about as strong as gnats' pee (weedy French gnats at that!). You'd have to swig the equivalent of half the English Channel for it to have any effect.

'God, it looks like you two have come to bury someone.' It's Tracy, wiggling past looking dead sexy (in a Shazzer sort of way), in a weeny white top and white skin-tight hipster jeans. I must admit I am feeling slightly overdressed. It's a hot day and the black certainly doesn't help. Merlin, of course, looks as cool as a corpse, but he is one of the living dead after all.

'Take a dekko at Laura's boobs,' he says far too loudly. 'Whoever designed her bra should have a go at that dodgy Millennium Bridge. It'd never wobble again.'

'I hope she doesn't go too near the barbecue, they'll end up grilled,' I add.

Just then Spike strides into the garden, holding a great big bunch of flowers, presumably for Laura.

'That's *very* not you,' said Merlin. 'I hope you're not trying to get off with Laura – I've got my eye on them – I mean *her*.'

'I came through the park. Someone had left them sticking out of the ground.'

Laura rushes over and grabs them.

'Oohh, Spike, how lovely, I've never been bought flowers before.'

'You still haven't,' I murmur under my breath.

'Why don't you let me show you round,' she adds, pulling poor Spike towards a sort of open shed at the end of their huge garden. I think they call it a gazebo or something.

'That's bloody unfair,' says Merlin. 'She's wasted on Spike.'

'Come on, Merlin, you're only after her body.'

'Oh, I see, so Spike's just going along to discuss the quantum theory?'

'I should think, with a body like hers, it's more likely to be relativity.'

'As long as it's not the Big Bang,' he adds gloomily. Merlin always beats me at words.

He mooches off to get another beer, skirting round the barbecue. I've hardly ever seen Merlin eat. He never has lunch at school and I've never seen any evidence of food in his dark domain except a few give-away toast crumbs. Some of us reckon he goes out late at night to bite virgins' necks. Mind you, he'd have to go a long way to find one in Northbridge – that's probably why he's so skinny. His favourite vampire film, by far, is that weirdo Roman Polanski's *Blood for Dracula*. I've had to watch it so many times I could be in it. Dracula (alias a bloke called Joe, strangely enough) turns up in New York because he can't get enough virgin's blood in Romania (he'd hate Northbridge!). He ends up sucking just about anything in a skirt, mind you!

'Hello, Joe, you came, then?' I turn round and it's Lucy something (I must find out her second name) looking dead cute and seriously babe-ular. She's had her long blonde hair cut straight at the back and she's wearing a short pink T-shirt dress with white trainers. She really has got great legs.

'Hi there, Lucy, how you doing? Been here long?' Phew, have I got chatting up babes licked – not!

'A bit too long – I find a whole load of girls together a bit scary.'

'Do you want a drink?'

'I'm all right, thanks. I've had a couple of Laura's specials. She apparently pinched a bottle of voddie out of her dad's sort of bar thing and shoved it in the fruit punch at the end of the garden. It's supposed to be non-alcoholic.'

'Sounds cool, but I won't go down there for the minute. She's just dragged Spike into her lair.'

'He brought her flowers, didn't he? Wasn't that sweet.'

'I doubt whether the park keeper would agree. He pinched them.'

She falls about laughing and as she leans forward I see she has the nicest boobs I've ever seen, even better than Debbie's from Cardiff in the Christmas *Razzle*. Normally I'm not really a breast man (unlike Merlin 'boobs' Labardia) – I'm more into legs, but catching a glimpse like that is a real turn-on.

Isn't it funny – seeing a girl's rude bits when you're not supposed to is so much more of a turn-on. I remember when we went to Spain once, we were on this beach where just about all the girls were topless. I found myself trying to glimpse the boobs of the only one wearing a top. Mind you, that's nothing. I once caught Merlin trying to peek through the arm hole of a dress on a shop dummy in the High Street. I told you he's a bit odd.

I sometimes wonder what it must be like going to bed with a girl with nothing on at all. I'd be like a kid let loose in a sweet shop, not knowing what to go for first. I don't suppose I'll ever find out – the rate I'm going.

'So how are you getting on in Northbridge? Where was it you came from? Chelmsford, wasn't it?'

'No, Brighton.'

'Ah, I knew it began with a B.'

She giggles (so far so good!). 'I'm afraid this place is a bit dreary after being there. My dad had to come here because of his job – he's an architect. Have you ever been to Brighton?'

'Yeah, last summer. I've got an uncle there.'

'Did you like it?'

'It was really cool, apart from this gay guy trying to pick me up on the front.'

'I don't blame him,' she says so quietly I can hardly hear. Then she blushes, giving the game away.

Blimey, isn't this a turn-up for the books? Two possible hits in just over a week. It's like old people say about buses – nothing for ages and then . . .

'Have you got a girlfriend, Joe?'

I think for a split second, and then realise I have absolutely nothing to hide.

'No, I'm a skeleton-free zone. Why, have you?'

'No, I haven't got a girlfriend either,' she says with a giggle. 'Sorry, bad joke. I suppose I have got someone really. He's in Brighton, but I don't get to see much of him.'

Here we go again.

'What's he like?'

'Oh, he's pretty good, but a bit of a fitness freak. It's football practice one evening, marathon practice the next. He goes windsurfing at the weekends and now he's talking about joining a gym. He never really has time for me. How about you? What sports are you into?'

'A bit of light darts once every four years, but I'm thinking of giving it up. I can't stand games – can't see the point. Everyone can beat me if they want. Merlin's the same.'

'What's Merlin like? Is he as weird as they all say?'

'Depends what you call weird. He seems pretty normal to me, but then maybe I'm a bit weird.'

'I don't think so. You just seem a bit of a loner – like you don't really fit in. I feel the same. I quite like the rest of these girls, but they don't seem to talk about anything but boys.'

'What do *you* like?'

'Oh, nothing special. I suppose the only thing I really like doing is watching old movies. That's terrible, isn't it?'

'Not at all. That's really funny – me and Merlin are obsessed with films. We're nuts about them. I want to be a director one day.'

'Honest? That's amazing. What's your favourite film ever?'

'It all depends. If it's funny – probably *Some Like it Hot*.'

'With Marilyn Monroe, Jack Lemmon and – er – Tony Curtis, wasn't it?'

'Blimey, you really do know films. What's yours?'

'Oh, I don't know. This week, anything with Harrison Ford in.'

'I think *Blade Runner*'s probably one of the best

films he ever did,' I say, trying to impress her.

'That's because it was directed by Ridley Scott who did *Gladiator*, he's the biz. Have you seen the director's cut?'

I'm completely blown away by this. A girl even knowing what a director is – whatever next? We carry on talking like this for what seems ages. Me trying to show off and Lucy coming back at me as if she knows what I'm going to say next.

Just then there's a little scream from the house. Laura's dad rushes in and drags out – you've guessed – Merlin, who's obviously found the punch and what looks like a rather large pink bikini top which he's wearing over his black T-shirt. It seems Laura had gone back from the garden only to find him rummaging through her laundry basket. Then he lunged at her, apparently.

I dash forward and volunteer to take him home. Laura's dad actually finds it quite funny, thank God, so no real harm's done. Just as I'm about to leave through the back gate I look back over my shoulder and see Lucy something giving me a rather sad little wave. Damn, I still don't know her second name.

The Labardia house.
Monday 8.30 a.m.

ACTION:

Well, what a funny old night that was. One minute my head's full of Jade, and whether I might stand a chance with her after all, and the next I'm thinking about Lucy. Jade – Lucy, Lucy – Jade, I just can't get my brain straight.

I call at the Bates Motel on the way to school but Merlin's not ready.

'I'm afraid he's not feeling his best today,' says Mrs Labardia with a knowing smile. 'He doesn't seem to remember much about yesterday, except something about trying to grab hold of some girl's rather ample chest and being thrown out. We even found a rather large bikini top hanging out of his pocket when we put him to bed. Thank you so much for bringing him home, Joe.'

I can't believe that family. If I was to arrive home drunk having been thrown out of a party for trying to fondle a girl's boobs I'd never hear the end of it. To them it seems like it happens every day. Merlin's right . . . he really is a lucky bastard.

'Morning, mate.' Merlin stumbles into the kitchen looking like death not even slightly warmed up. 'Excuse me if I don't talk, my tongue's like a big, furry rat – a big, *dead* furry rat.'

'Your mum says you don't remember much about yesterday?'

'I can't even remember what I'm not supposed to remember much about. I just have some vague memory of Laura's top but I can't think why.'

'Could it be because you were wearing it?'

'Really? Oh lord – how did I look?'

'Well, you'll never make Page Three.'

'That's all right, they don't wear anything on Page Three. Anyway, what happened to you? I hardly saw you all afternoon.'

'I was talking to that Lucy bird. The one from Brighton. She's really cool. She's into films in a big way.'

Merlin smiles strangely and then puts his head in his hands and pretends to cry.

Mrs Labardia comes back into the kitchen.

'Do you want any breakfast, Merlin? It's getting a bit late for school.'

'No thanks, Ma. I don't suppose I could have a couple of pints of lager instead?'

Mrs Labardia laughs and pours him a glass of orange juice.

'I think you'd better not drink anything remotely alcoholic until next Saturday.'

Mr Labardia strolls into the kitchen carrying the paper. He turns to me. 'Hi, man, how you doing?'

'Fine thanks, Mr Labardia.'

Merlin and the girls call their parents by their Christian names, but I can't – even though they ask me to.

'Did you get pissed like young Casanova here?'

'Not really, I'm still recovering from my sister's wedding.'

'What about you, Merlin? I take it you weren't drinking *that* stuff.' He points to the orange juice rather disapprovingly.

'No, Father, there was this nasty woman there, who forced poisoned fruit punch down my throat. There was nothing I could do.'

'She wouldn't be the one you tried to molest by any remote chance?'

'I believe I might just have slipped and grabbed the nearest things to me.'

Sky dashes into the breakfast-room. 'Hell, I'm really late. Hi, Joe, how you doing? Upset anyone else lately?'

'Who, me? What do you mean?'

'Well, I'm not sure what you said to Jade yesterday, but she seems well pissed off.' She gives Merlin a huge theatrical wink and throws a slice of bread into the toaster.

'We'd better go,' he says. 'I'm staying out of this.'

Once we're out on the street, Merlin turns to me.

'It looks like your plan really worked. Jade's never ever been given the cold shoulder before – she's pretty mad. Well done, mate.'

'Oh yeah, fat lot of good it does me. By the way, what was that funny little smile for, when I told you that Lucy's really into movies?'

'I said I wouldn't say anything, but she came up to me last week and said she really liked you. She even asked what you were really into. I told her all about your sister's marriage to that silly Bunt and about our movie and about the films you liked most.'

'Jesus, devious or what?' I say, feeling a bit as if I've been had.

'Don't go off on one, Joe. I told her you were feeling a bit fed up. She obviously wanted to impress you.'

'She must have done a lot of homework.'

'No, she is really interested in movies anyway, honest. She actually does know quite a lot.'

'What do you think of her?'

'I think she seems pretty cool. Looks a bit like that bird who plays Buffy – not really my type, not big enough, if you know what I mean – but dead pretty, in an untouchable sort of way.'

'You don't fancy her because she might be a vampire slayer.'

Merlin laughed. 'Good point. Are you going to see her again?'

'Depends on Jade, really.'

Merlin stops dead in his tracks and looks directly into my eyes.

'Look, Joe, just because Jade's a bit pissed off because you don't appear to be lusting after her, it doesn't necessarily mean she feels any differently about going out with you. You gave her ego a jolt, and neither of my sisters are used to that.'

'So you think if I really told her how I felt – love and all that – she'd feel better, but then walk away just the same.'

'I'd bet my life on it, mate. Look, you're calling the shots at the moment, why don't you just sit back and enjoy it? You've always got that Lucy to fall back on.'

Hang on a minute. It's funny, but I suddenly don't really like the idea of poor Lucy as a second string – she's worth far more than that. I mean, how would I feel if someone told me I was first reserve? I reckon the best thing is to let things go at their own pace like Merlin says. Anyway, compared to how I felt this time last week, things are almost approaching the shady side of not bad.

Scene 18

Northbridge Video.
Saturday 9.30 p.m.

ACTION:

It's Saturday and I'm at work.

I really, really, really don't know how I feel about the Labardias' anniversary party tonight. I'm not really into parties that much at the best of times, but I have to say theirs are usually quite a riot. Mum and Dad – those-who-must-be-obeyed – said I could stop over if I want and Merlin says he's only asked the very best people along. As I said earlier, whenever the Labardias have a bash they always let their kids have one of their own. Cool or what?

I suppose the real problem is that I know I'll see Jade and I haven't a clue how to deal with it. If I carry on being dead cool, sure I'll walk away with my ego intact, but without the girl (or any part of the girl) – and that's a dead cert. If I let her know how I really feel, on the other hand, she'll run a mile and probably laugh her head off while she's doing it. It's heads I lose, tails I lose too. The only thing I *can* do is let *her* do all the running. If she wants me, she can have me – but she'll have to ask nicely (ish).

And if all that's not registering high enough on the difficult scale, I think I've got a class A spot coming, right next to my nose. It's one of those that starts with a vague itch and then mutates into an alien being with a mind of its own. The only thing I can hope is that it'll still only be a toddler alien by this evening. Anyway, Merlin's room's so dark you'll be lucky to see my old nose let alone a new one.

I'm back at the video shop, so I know I won't be able to think about IT or much else until later. I've only been here for a few minutes when the manager calls me over.

'Joe, do you know anything about the movie *Father of the Bride*?'

I look across and there's an old dear standing at the counter.

'What, the Steve Martin one?' (There was one made in the Fifties with Spencer Tracy.)

'Yeah! This lady wants to know if there's any sex in it?'

I look at her but can't quite decide whether she'd want there to be or not.

'Afraid not. It's just about this guy in America whose wife and daughter want a really posh wedding but he wants to do it on the cheap. It's pretty funny.'

(It's even funnier when I think of my dad still griping about the cut-price wedding he gave Zoe.)

'Is there any fighting or shooting?'

She obviously isn't a big Steve Martin fan – Rambo he most certainly isn't.

'None at all, I'm afraid.'

'That's the trouble with the films these days,' she says, not remotely paying attention to what I've just said. 'They're all sex and violence. Now when I was young they made films about nice things. Now that Bing Crosby . . .'

Time to head her off at the pass, as they say in the best cowboy films. I break in as I can see the manager needs to get on.

'I think you'll like this one a lot. I don't think there's even any swearing in it.'

'Are you sure?'

I feel like saying 'Of course I'm bloody sure,' but think better of it. Actually it was Zoe's favourite film and one of the lamest Steve Martin ever made, but I wasn't going to tell her that. Maybe I should suggest *Scream 3*, that would teach her to listen to me.

The customers we get are really stupid. Quite often it seems like they want me to promise that they're going to like a film, like a sort of guarantee. I bet they're the same with anything else they buy, come to that.

'Are you sure Doreen and I are going to enjoy a holiday paddling up the Orinoko in a dugout canoe?'

'Are you certain my teenage son's going to like Barry Manilow's new CD?'

'Is this shade of lipstick *really* going to make all men want to kiss me?' . . .

On the other hand, in our shop lots of people only read the title to decide what a film's about – and then complain when it isn't what they thought. So you get some thinking that *The Silence of the Lambs* is a film about a deaf sheep farmer, or *Moby Dick* is about a guy who can't get a hard-on. I'm joking, but you know what I mean. I remember some guy giving me a hard time because he took out *Kiss of the Spider Woman* thinking it was a girlie version of *Spiderman* only to find out it was about two blokes having it off in jail.

The morning's pretty ordinary until . . .

'Hi, Joe.'

It's Lucy something (I really must find out her second name), followed by big Laura and rude Tracy, who's cruising the adult videos at the far end of the store and giggling.

'How's it going? Did you get Merlin back all right last Sunday? I missed you at school this week.'

'Just about, thanks. How's things with you, Lucy? Oh, hi there, Laura.'

Laura speaks right over Lucy. 'We just came in to ask if you know anything about Merlin's "do" this evening?'

'I didn't know you were going. I haven't a clue how many people Merlin's asked. The Labardias' parties are usually pretty cool though.'

'I'm going to have to tell my dad it's at someone else's after last Sunday.'

'Did you get your top back?'

'No, Merlin said I could have it back tonight, but only if he could fit it.'

'Like Cinderella and the slipper.'

'Sort of,' she giggles.

'Oh, I shouldn't worry about him, he'll have his own bra by now. His parents buy him everything. Are you coming tonight, Lucy?'

'Merlin asked me, but I don't think my parents will let me. They've heard a few strange stories about his mum and dad.'

'Oh, they're all right – just a bit different. Listen, I can't really talk now – it's getting busy – I'll catch you later.'

I feel ever so relieved that Lucy isn't going to Merlin's party. At least that should leave me free to sort the Jade thing out.

As they leave I cop a swift glance at Lucy as she walks away. Cute little bum, brilliant legs, skin-tight jeans, T-shirt, and one of those silly little rucksacks that you can just about get a Tampax in. Still, eh! Nobody's perfect.

Home again.

Luckily my new spot shows no further signs of eruption. It must still be going through its dormant phase. Mind you, if it *was* a volcano, all the people living on the edges of it would be packing their bags and making for the foothills by now. It always amazes me where spots come from. It's like they're creeping around inside your body trying to decide where to break out next.

The other trouble with my head is that my hair's got a bit long and is beginning to stick up. I'm beginning to look like Gary Rhodes, or that Jim Carey (the plonker in *The Mask*) who is *so* who I don't want to look like. Still, at least I don't have a face like a foam rubber puppet like him. I decide to use the stuff that I bought months ago to bleach my hair, and make it all spikey with gel. Mum and Dad will do their nuts, but I'm past caring.

I still haven't worked out when's best to turn up at parties. If you arrive too late all the girls you might want to pull are taken, but if you arrive too early you have to talk to parents and stuff. Mind you, if you've got to talk to any, they might as well be Merlin's. It's nine o'clock now and I'm still wondering what time to go.

'Aren't you going to your party, dear? It's gone nine. It'll all be over before you get there, if you don't hurry.'

Guess who's at my door? Zulu alert!

I can't open it. If she sees my hair she'll go spare. I look in the mirror. Jeez, it looks really cool.

'It's all right, Mummy,' I say in a little voice, 'I decided I'd miss the conjuror and the free balloons and just turn up for the jelly.'

'You'll miss *all* the food at this rate.'

Rover perks up at the mention of food.

It's dead odd. Have you noticed that when people get old and are no longer on the pull, all they ever think about is where their next meal's coming from?

When they get to a party they always seem to check out first that there's an ample supply of grub before they can think of anything else. It's like a security blanket. I quickly check my room for naked movie stars and open the door a couple of centimetres.

'Don't worry, Mum, I won't need food – drugs take your appetite away.'

'Now look here, I know what those Labardias are like. If you think we're going to let you kil–'

'J for joke, Ma,' I groan. 'Anyway, I've already had my fix this evening.'

'I'm glad you *can* joke about such things. Look at that poor Carter girl from Sunnydale Crescent, she's now living in a down-and-outs hostel in Brixton.'

'That's probably got more to do with Sunnydale Crescent than drugs,' I say, almost *meaning* it.

'And I don't want you coming home drunk and disgracing us.'

'It's all right, Ma. If you remember, it's an away match – I'm not coming home at all. I can disgrace myself round their house.'

'I really don't know. When I was your age I . . .'

'Thank you, Mother, and goodnight,' I say, gently closing the door. All I need at the moment is another 'when I was your age' lecture.

Scene 19

The Labardias' party.
Saturday 9.30 p.m.

ACTION:

'Joe, darling, how simply divine to see you.' It's Merlin's rather drunken mum who meets me at the door, done up like a mermaid. 'You must come through and see what we've done, before you go up to Merlin's party.'

If the Labardia house is usually what you might call weird, tonight it looks like a home for deranged interior decorators. The theme, for no reason I can think of, is 'Atlantis, City of the Deep'. In their church-hall sized front room, large papier mâché fish are dangling from the ceilings and a machine in the corner is chucking out millions of coloured bubbles. Special tanks have been hired, full of brilliant darting fish and the floor has been sprinkled with sand and shells. Long, damp traily things also hang from the ceiling to look like seaweed and all the drinks are bright green and sort of luminous. Weirdest of all is the wavy lighting, which makes everyone look seasick (and probably feel it too).

Jane Labardia can hardly walk owing to a long, green, shiny, leg-clinging tube which tapers to a tail trailing along behind her. She's painted her top half green, sprinkled herself in glitter and put two rather too-small shells on her two rather too-large boobs. Her green hair seems to be made of real seaweed which hangs slimily all the way down her back and pongs ever so slightly of fish.

Tony Labardia, Merlin's dad, has come as an octopus. His eight arms, which are all waving about, appear to be hollow and he has made the costume so that he can choose which ones he puts his real ones in. Why? I soon notice the more scantily-dressed female guests trying to guess which of the arms are currently 'occupied'. Those are the ones that Merlin's dad is using to grope them with. At the moment he's managed to get both his good tentacles around a monster shrimp. Unfortunately it turns out to be a bloke shrimp, but neither seems to mind that much.

I, myself, have always and will always hate fancy dress. Call me a spoilsport if you like, but the idea of spending the whole evening looking a total prat (or in this case sprat), while the guys who decided not to bother get off with the best babes, seems daft to me. I mean, you're hardly going to pull done up like a kipper, are you?

Luckily Merlin feels the same (or so I'd presumed) and as I enter his domain I see he's ignored the underwater theme. His dungeon has only changed by the fact that the cobwebs and the stuffed ex-pets are lit up by hundreds of little candles. When I'm in there, I seem to make out about ten to fifteen bodies lounging around on the floor in a cloud of smoke.

'Want some wacky baccy, Joe?' asks Merlin, who for some reason has dressed as Marlene Dietrich and is carrying a long cigarette holder. (See! I was right about him having his own bra by now.)

'No thanks, sweetie,' I reply nicely. I've always suffered mildly from asthma so any sort of smoking sets me off.

'Suit yourself, daaaarling. Let me introduce you to my sister Jade,' he says in a rather soppy voice and then wiggles over to the other side of the room. Actually he looks rather good in a blonde wig and a dress – I hope this isn't a sign of things to come.

I kneel down and feel myself trembling in anticipation.

'Hi, Joe, I hoped you'd be here,' Jade says in her low, sexy voice. 'Have you done something to your hair? It looks really good.'

She places a candle between us and I struggle to keep my eyes on her face as I take in what she's wearing. Seriously, if her top was cut any lower there'd be no point. In the half light I notice a small tattoo of a dolphin on her right boob (that's her right, my left, if you're fussy). I can't work out whether it's real or just for the party. She leans forward and kisses me lightly on the cheek.

'I – I sort of hoped you'd be here too,' I burble. 'I mean, I knew you'd be here but I didn't . . .'

'I know what you mean, Joe. It's lovely to see you, I just didn't know if you liked me any more after last

Sunday. If you still do, I thought we might disappear to my room a bit later for a talk and things.'

The Angel of Cool has returned to my shoulder and is screaming BE BLOODY CAREFUL in my ear. After due consideration, at least a fraction of a millisecond, I decide he can piss off as far as I'm concerned.

'I don't just *like* you, Jade, I'm actually in lo–'

At that precise second I glance up and see Lucy something staring at me from across the gloom.

'You actually what, Joe?' Jade whispers, stroking my cheek.

'I – er – actually . . . was on my way for a pee. Sorry, I'll be back in a sec.'

I reverse out of the room to where Merlin has his own bathroom (the only bathroom with a black bog and bath I've ever seen). I don't know what it is about lavatory seats, but I seem to be making a habit of sitting on them to think.

Shit! Sod! Damn! Bugger! What the hell is Lucy doing here, for Christ's sake? She said she wasn't going to be able to come. Just as I'm about to disprove everything Merlin said, I see that silly moo staring at me with that little girl lost face. I should just ignore her and get on with it. Go to Jade's room and go all the way if she'll let me. ALL THE BLOODY WAY! This could be the biggest night of my life – the end of girlie mags – the beginning of grown-updom. I could have the best-looking babe in the land and be a hero among all red-blooded males.

So why am I sitting here on a lavatory seat leaving Jade alone for someone else to pick up? Why aren't I out there giving it plenty? I suppose, when it really comes down to it, I wonder if I'm actually fully prepared to go through with it? I mean . . .

What if I'm really crap?

What if nothing happens in the old willie department?

What if Jade is *really* experienced and just makes me look stupid?

What if it's all over in seconds? Jesus, I've practised enough, but not 'in the field' so to speak.

What if she tells all her friends I'm a no-no?

What if it gets all round school that Joe Derby – alias Mr Cool – can't actually do it?

What if Lucy gets to hear?

SHIT! WHAT IF LUCY GETS TO HEAR?

It's no good, I realise I can't go through with it, even if there is anything to go through with. I feel like the young guy in *American Pie* who has to hire someone else to do it for him. I'm just going to have to wait. If Jade Labardia really fancies me, then she'll have to bloody wait too – till I'm ready.

I walk slowly downstairs out into the back garden which is all twinkly, with tiny white lights set into the trees.

'Hello, Joe, I wondered if you'd come out here.'

This time I think it's going to be Jade but find myself hoping it's Lucy.

It IS Lucy – sitting alone on a bench looking dead pretty!

'I heard that you and Jade Labardia were having a bit of a thing.'

'Who told you that, was it Merlin?'

'Spike told Laura last Sunday. Is it true, Joe? I don't blame you. She is very beautiful.'

'I'm not sure I really fancy her, Lucy.' (OK, I'm lying, but sometimes the truth can be somewhat overrated.) 'To be honest,' I continue, 'I've been thinking of you quite a lot of the time since Sunday.'

Lucy leans forward, closes her eyes and kisses me with her mouth open. Our teeth clash a bit but who cares? Enough practise and we'll soon get the hang of it.

Just then, over her shoulder, I glimpse Jade and Sky Labardia, the infamous double act, leading a couple of older guys I've never seen before into the shrubbery at the end of the garden. I think about it logically. Whoever said it first got it in one: a bird in the hand is most certainly worth two in the bush.

'Do you know, Lucy,' I say quietly, 'I don't even know your second name.'

She hesitates for a bit and then, with a huge giggle, whispers, 'Bunt.'

If you would like more information about
books available from Piccadilly Press and how
to order them, please contact us at:

Piccadilly Press Ltd.
5 Castle Road
London
NW1 8PR

Tel: 020 7267 4492
Fax: 020 7267 4493

Feel free to visit our website at
www.piccadillypress.co.uk